W.R.A.I.T.H.

BY

ADAM LOWE

With thanks to my parents for their
support and encouragement
to keep going.

Published 2022

The author acknowledges Ruth Lowe as editor and
contributor to this book.

www.wraithbookman.wixsite.com/wraith-books

ISBN: 9798819556061

Imprint: Independently published

FOREWORD

The author Adam Lowe began to write his first book W.R.A.I.T.H. as a young teenager. Leaving it, then returning to it again and again over several years; adding layers to the characters and his own creative illustrations, the story evolved over time with a series to the first book already in progress.

Taking inspiration from other writers such as Ian Fleming, John Buchan and screenwriter/director Christopher McQuarrie, the story W.R.A.I.T.H came to life in Adam's imagination. The attributes of the protagonist, Fergus McIntyre, developed from a combination of traits seen in well-known fictional characters, such as the calm woodenness of Bond to the intuitive mind and derring-do of former intelligence officer Richard Hannay. Adam also took inspiration for his character from the courage, bravery, and determination of real-life Scottish freedom fighter William Wallace.

W.R.A.I.T.H., proposes to revert back to the reasons why spy stories were told, with issues that tackle current world problems. The book also highlights how the wars of the past still affect us today. Fortunately, we have not reached another world war - yet, but the threat is always there.

Warfare has moved into the digital age; cyber-attacks are more frequent and military use robotic drones to infiltrate enemy lines. Controlling the masses and what they think is managed by propaganda media and surveillance systems. Although with all this technology you would think the world has moved forward and yet we still have narcissistic dictators who have their fingers on the big red button. This combination makes our world a very dangerous place.

A desire to solve the mystery of who is behind global criminal networks and to rid the world of such oppressors is a motive that Fergus McIntyre will carry throughout a series of W.R.A.I.T.H. books.

CONTENTS

'OUR ALLIES ARE
OUR ENEMIES'

CHAPTER ONE

RIO DE JANEIRO

A cacophony of sound polluted the air. Blaring car horns, construction machinery, samba music, barking dogs and angry commuters yelled at each other while making their way through the city streets. Rio de Janeiro, like every other day, bustled with life. A city of colour and vibrance, dance and carnivals, from dawn to dusk there was never a quiet moment.

On the high ground surrounding the city, little tin and brick houses built on top of each other sprawled into the distance. Children ran in between the alleyways practicing their football skills, hopeful of being selected as the next star for their country's national team. All seemed normal as the Carioca people carried on their normal daily routine.

Three large black SUVs made their way through the Favela streets. They stopped in a plaza encased by hundreds of makeshift houses.

Outstepped a dark-skinned man with a marksman rifle. He was a former R.U.F member, now a wanted terrorist, code-named the Cobra.

The Cobra entered a house and made his way up a staircase. Eventually he reached a flat roof and placed a nitro cell gently down by his feet.

In the plaza below the Cobra's henchmen stood guard with their guns loaded and ready for any conflict.

The Cobra knelt down and aimed his rifle at his target. He held his gun tighter, took precision aim and gently curved his finger around the trigger.

....

About half a mile away a meeting was taking place with various United Nation members and heads of state. Attending the meeting was the British Prime Minister, The First Minister of

Scotland and the President of the United States of America.

The British Prime Minister stood up from his chair, prepared himself to make his speech and cleared his throat. As he gathered his papers a small red light appeared on his chest. Suddenly the light travelled upwards and a round of shots fired on the wall behind him.

Everyone in the room quickly dropped to the floor to take cover, except for two bodyguards who rushed to the Prime Ministers aid.

. . . .

The Cobra had missed his target. Instead, he found himself wrestling over his rifle with a strange man.

The stranger was wearing an entirely black suit and was well built. He had a gruff look about him. A reddish-brown beard covered most of his face and his blue eyes flashed angrily the Cobra. He was clearly an expert in combat and displayed skills only military personnel would be trained in. The stranger grabbed the rifle barrel, swung it round and attempted to hit the Cobra's head with the gun's buttstock.

The Cobra managed to dodge the blow then swiftly reached into his pocket and withdrew a detonating device.

The stranger immediately moved back.

The Cobra smiled coolly at the stranger then pressed a button on the device. Suddenly the there was a loud explosion and the roof crumbled and collapsed under their feet.

The men fell into a stairwell. Clouds of dust and debris filled the air. The Cobra stood up, blood and dust covered his face. He looked across the hall. The stranger stood opposite, mirroring his image.

Turning around the Cobra quickly ran down the staircase. On reaching the next landing he smashed through a window and barrel rolled out onto a scrap metal roof at the back of the building. The stranger continued to chase after him.

Descending before them the rooftops of the Favela resembled a ramshackle staircase, each unsteady step taking them further down the hillside. Narrow gaps between the houses made it easy for them to leap from house to house and street to street. Each jump they made onto the metal corrugated rooftops rumbled loudly like thunder and reverberated through the maze of houses.

The Cobra jumped down from a roof on to the road below, then ran into a sheltered market on the edge of the Favela.

The stranger, tracking close behind, held up a gun and took aim at the Cobra and shot him in the leg. The Cobra stumbled to the ground and looked up to see his attacker. He felt a strong grip and twist on his shoulder. The stranger then spun him around and knocked him out with one punch. With ease the stranger dragged the Cobra's unconscious body across the dirty market floor and threw him off the edge of a Favela terrace.

On the road below, a few meters down, a man and a woman sat quietly in the front seats of a Range Rover. A gentle breeze passed through their open sunroof.

Suddenly there was an almighty bang as the Cobra's body came crashing through the sunroof. The man and woman jumped in their seats and turned around.

Climbing down from the terrace the stranger walked over to the Range Rover and opened the door. The woman in the car spoke to the stranger.

"Fergus! Are you alright?" she asked anxiously.

"It's just a spot of blood Turner," replied the stranger.

The stranger then acknowledged the man in the driver's seat. "Collier," he said bluntly.

"McIntyre," replied Collier with the same amount of directness.

They nodded to each other, then together the two men hauled the Cobra's body further into the backseat of the car.

McIntyre - the stranger - slumped back in his seat and exhaustedly said one word.

"Drive."

CHAPTER TWO

THE AMAZON RAINFOREST

Days had passed from the attack in Rio. It was all over the headlines on the news. McIntyre, Turner and Collier, along with their hostage the Cobra, were taking shelter in a small village in the rainforest by the Amazon River.

Although their location was isolated, it wasn't very peaceful. Loud chirps and whoops could be heard from unidentified creatures of the forest and there was a constant humming and thrumming from insects communicating to one another. Apart from the beasts around them no one knew that in this ordinary little wooden house was the most wanted man in Brazil.

"Who the hell are you?!" yelled McIntyre interrogating the Cobra.

"No one ever told me that you Brits were so… foolish," said the Cobra smugly.

McIntyre, losing patience, grabbed the Cobra by his collar.

"Tell me why you were in Rio, and why you targeted that meeting!" shouted McIntyre in the Cobra's face.

"Let's just say, if I tell you, you will change your mind and turn to our side," answered the Cobra.

McIntyre then slammed his hand down onto a table and let out a long-frustrated sigh.

"You can slam your hand down on that table until it breaks, but you don't scare me. It's kind of funny though. Do it again," the Cobra said sniggering.

"Fine, we'll do baby steps then, shall we? Let's start with your name. Your real name!" shouted McIntyre.

The Cobra sighed. "Fine, it's Demarco Adebayo," he said finally confessing.

There was a loud crack from a gunshot and a bullet penetrated the wooden house, just skimming McIntyre's shoulder. McIntyre quickly ran round the back of Adebayo, then using Adebayo as a shield McIntyre escorted him out of the room while pointing a gun over Adebayo's shoulder.

It had gone very quiet. Even the birds had stopped their chattering.

Then suddenly there was a flurry of bullets and splinters flying through the house. McIntyre and Adebayo ducked down for cover. They reached the wooden doorway and McIntyre took a quick glance outside. He could see several of Adebayo's henchmen firing rapidly with their AK rifles.

"What the hell is going on?" shouted Collier.

"Just stay down!" McIntyre shouted back at Collier who was taking shelter under a table with Turner.

The gunfire finally stopped. For a split-second McIntyre was distracted. Adebayo took this opportunity to escape, he elbowed McIntyre in the ribs and made for the door. Adebayo then ran out the house and escaped into the forest.

McIntyre sighed, "I am really sick of chasing that guy."

Before McIntyre could stand up a grenade flew through an open window and rolled on to the mud floor in front of him.

Instantly McIntyre jumped up and ran through the doorway. There was a huge explosion. Rubble, splinters, and ash blasted up into the air and the house burst into flames. He looked behind briefly, then ran at full speed into the forest after Adebayo.

Weaving their way through the forest the men ran over giant tree roots and vines. The dense undergrowth on the forest floor made it difficult to run and fern branches sliced into their skin as they ploughed their way through. The gunshot Adebayo had received in his leg days before hindered his escape and allowed McIntyre to catch up with him.

Adebayo then stopped abruptly and looked down. He had reached a cliff edge above a river ravine. He turned to face McIntyre.

"Nowhere to run now! Huh?!" shouted McIntyre confident he had his opponent cornered.

"I think you'll find that's wrong," Adebayo answered. He walked closer to the edge, leaned back slowly, and looked up at the sky.

"NO!!" yelled McIntyre as he ran forward.

But it was too late. Adebayo disappeared off the edge of the cliff. McIntyre stood shaking his head in disbelief, no one would ever survive that fall.

Standing at the cliff edge McIntyre could hear the fire at the house crackling in the distance. He ran back to the house and saw the entire structure burning in an orange inferno. The Range Rover that they had arrived in was also on fire. That confirmed one disturbing truth in his mind. Turner and Collier were dead.

CHAPTER THREE

MI5 HQ, THAMES HOUSE, LONDON

Millbank was quiet on that morning when their deadliest assassin arrived for work.

McIntyre walked the long corridors in silence. Escorting him was a tall security guard who marched in front leading the way. McIntyre felt uncomfortable. Everyone was staring at him like he was some kind of monster, as if he himself had killed Turner and Collier.

Eventually he arrived at the head of M.I.5's office only to realise someone else was waiting for him. McIntyre stood still in the doorway. He nodded at his boss the Director General then addressed the other man.

"Mr Home Secretary," said McIntyre edgily. He anticipated he about to get a dressing-down and took a deep breath.

"Come in McIntyre," said the Home Secretary. "I do hope you understand that what happened in Rio set us back enormously. The Prime Minister wants answers. The U.N. wants you sacked and the S.A.S. …." He paused for a moment, then turned to face McIntyre "…well you can imagine what they want to do to you."

The Home Secretary continued. "Let's not dwell on the past shall we. You're the best we have, and you have another task ahead. We want you to stop off at Lake Garda and then head to Venice. You will be given instructions when you get there.

The Home Secretary sat down on a leather wingback chair opposite the Director Generals desk.

The Director General then began to instruct McIntyre. "You will need to travel low profile as you are a dead man McIntyre. I hope you realise how much pressure is on us, so you need to get this right for both our sakes."

15

"We are in an intelligence war McIntyre." Now go to war." the Director General finally instructed.

"Yes Sir. Thank you, Sir." replied McIntyre, relieved he was let off so lightly. He left the room and started preparing for his next mission.

CHAPTER FOUR

ISOLA DEL GARDA, LAKE GARDA, ITALY

It was a blindingly beautiful day and a warm breeze flowed in the air. The hull of a small motorboat sliced through the lake's crystal blue water and headed towards an island, lush with exotic plants and tall cypress trees.

Through the vegetation a large gothic villa came into view. McIntyre docked his boat at a small jetty on the island and made his way to the beautiful gardens.

Directly in front of him, standing perfectly straight was a butler. He was quite well built and dressed in a black tailored suit. His silver, grey hair was slicked back with hair cream, and he wore a perfectly groomed moustache.

The butler spoke directly to McIntyre. "Lovely summer day isn't it. Summer is my favourite season."

"I prefer Autumn, it's a good time to feed the ducks." replied McIntyre.

"Good to see you Sir." said the Butler extending his hand to McIntyre.

"It's good to see you too Benson." replied McIntyre.

They smiled and shook hands then continued to walk slowly through the gardens.

"So, where exactly am I?" McIntyre asked.

"You are at the Isola del Garda, or as some people call it 'The Pearl of the Lake'. Once used by monks and as a refuge for smugglers. It is now the home of the Cavazza family who only use it in the winter. They have kindly rented it as a safehouse," explained Benson.

McIntyre and Benson made their way to the entrance.

As Benson reached out his hand to open the door, he suddenly remembered some information. "Oh, I almost forgot Sir, your Quartermaster was replaced."

"By whom?" asked McIntyre.

"Oh, you'll see." said Benson as he unlocked the door of the main entrance.

Benson opened the doors and together they walked inside into a large grand hallway. Suddenly bass music started to boom out from a stereo system on the sideboard.

A man wearing a multi-coloured jacket, white trousers, basketball boots and a flat baseball cap came dancing down the stairs.

"Who the hell is this?" McIntyre asked Benson.

"This Sir" said Benson "is Kody Woods. Your new Quartermaster. He's quite a character."

"WOO HOO!!" Woods yelled as he jumped down the last few steps.

"MASTER WOODS!!" shouted Benson trying to introduce McIntyre over the booming music. "THIS IS MCINTYRE!!!"

"WHAT!! I CAN'T HEAR YOU OVER THIS SICK BEAT! IT'S GOOD RIGHT!" Woods shouted back.

Benson went over to turn off the ear-splitting music.

"Master Woods, this is McIntyre." said Benson calmly.

McIntyre and Woods shook hands.

"Alright!" Woods said in a loud long drawn-out American accent.

Woods misinterpreted McIntyre's friendly handshake and proceeded to give him a hug.

McIntyre, feeling uncomfortable, pushed Woods away.

"Erm … Hello Woods." replied McIntyre and he moved further back.

McIntyre then looked at Benson and silently expressed his dislike for Woods.

Benson responded by shrugging his shoulders and rolled his eyes in exasperation.

"You got my Bartle Skeet?" Woods asked Benson.

"Yes Sir." replied Benson. He left the room and promptly returned carrying a silver plate with two cocktail glasses and a soda can balanced on it.

"Ahhhh." sighed Woods happily. There was a loud hiss as he opened a can, then he poured the bright, lime green liquid into the two cocktail glasses.

"Want some?" Woods asked McIntyre and offered him a glass.

"No thanks." McIntyre replied through gritted teeth and wondered why anyone would drink a soft drink from a cocktail glass.

"Ah, that's right, I forgot, you're a man of getting down to business. More for me then." said Woods. He then started to sip loudly out of both glasses.

Woods walked toward the staircase carrying his drinks. "I'll lead the way." he said.

McIntyre and Benson followed Woods up the stairs.

McIntyre leaned towards Benson and whispered "I see what you mean about the character thing. Maybe it's all that caffeine he's drinking."

Benson mumbled and nodded in agreement.

Woods, Benson and McIntyre walked along the upper corridors of the mansion. It was like an exhibition. Every inch of every wall was covered in works of art. Bodies of armour and marble busts stood proud on either side of the corridor.

"Pretty cool, huh." said Woods. "You know the Italian renaissance was in the 15th and 16th century and they called it the Quattrocento and Cinquecento period, this was when they were kinda transitioning out of Middle Ages."

McIntyre and Benson looked at Woods in surprise.

"What! I'm not a total doofus you know." said Woods a little put out. "Come on." he said and continued to walk down the corridor.

Finally, they stopped at a vault door.

"You're gonna like this." said Woods to McIntyre.

Woods opened the door, turned around and said in a loud voice "Take it away Benson!"

They entered the room. It was dark inside except for several illuminated display cabinets which overflowed with weapons of every kind imaginable.

"This is the Armoury room Sir." said Benson. He took McIntyre over to a cabinet containing a selection of Sub-machine guns and removed one of them.

"Beretta PMX Sir, snappy little thing this is." said Benson coolly, his face half shadowed in the dim light.

"Oooooooh that's a good one man." Woods said excitedly.

"Perfect for you Sir." said Benson handing it to McIntyre.

Benson opened a drawer underneath the cabinet which had a number of small, black military briefcases. He searched in the drawer and removed one of the cases. Inside were the magazines for the gun.

"Armour piercing titanium bullets Sir. This'll get through anything." said Benson picking a bullet up and showing it to McIntyre like it was an exhibition piece.

"This guy knows his s#*t dude." Woods interrupted crudely.

Benson and McIntyre both turned to look at Woods and shook their heads. Woods feeling their displeasure then slowly turned away and entertained himself.

Benson returned the magazine of bullets back into the case. He then guided McIntyre through another doorway into a fitting room. Five jackets were hung on display. Benson gestured to McIntyre to choose one.

"This one." McIntyre said pointing to a black jacket with a shiny texture.

"Ah, excellent choice Sir. This is what I call the Raven. It has bullet-proofed aramid fibre sewn into the lining of the jacket, giving you a flexible but strong armour. I'll get this rolled up for you right away." said Benson.

"In the meantime, why don't you come with me and see the real party." said Woods feeling left out.

Woods led McIntyre back into the Armoury. He walked over to a desk in the middle of the room and bent down to look into a cabinet.

"Just a second." said Woods then he presented McIntyre with a large black metal discus.

"What's that?" asked McIntyre.

"It's an underwater explosive." Woods replied. "I just thought might need it given where you are going. I mean this bad boy is amazing."

Woods showed McIntyre a small device.

"This is the detonator. You push the red button for it to activate. Obvs." Woods said rolling his eyes.

Woods then laid out two small, yellow blocks, each one fitted with a small screen.

"These are DNA scanners. We have already uploaded several known terrorists. All you need to do is type in a name, and voilà! You've got em. I like the colour of them, don't you?" Woods asked excitedly.

McIntyre stared at Woods without answering him then packed all the gadgets into a briefcase.

Benson came out the fitting room with another briefcase containing the guns and the Raven jacket.

He walked towards a wall at the far end of the room and pressed on it firmly. There was a small click. A secret door opened revealing a dark and dusty stairwell. On the walls were bulkhead lamps covered in cobwebs. It was obvious nobody had used this passage for a while.

Benson flicked a switch and turned the lights on, he entered the doorway then one by one the men descended the stairs.

They reached a tunnelled canal with a Riva Aquarama super boat berthed at the canal bank.

Benson placed both briefcases into the boat.

"You're probably expecting me to know how much horsepower this thing has. All I know is it's a boat and there's a lot of them where you are going. I do however know a bit about this tunnel. It was used by the Germans and Italians in World War Two to help them escape out of northern Italy undetected." explained Woods.

McIntyre looked again in surprise at Woods.

Woods snapped at him, "Ok you gotta stop doing that every time I mention something of historical interest."

Benson then briefed McIntyre on his journey.

"Your route will take you from here to Verona through ancient underground tunnels. Then on through several small open canals connected to the Adige River. Eventually you'll reach another underground tunnel, this will lead you to Venice. A guidance system is in your briefcase."

McIntyre stepped into the boat and familiarised himself with the controls.

"Safe travels Sir." said Benson.

McIntyre didn't say anything but nodded his head to gesture goodbye. He turned the engine on which made a quiet purring noise. Turning the steering wheel slowly he guided the boat into the middle of the canal.

"Send me a postcard!" shouted Woods. His voice echoed off the walls as McIntyre disappeared down the long dark tunnel.

CHAPTER FIVE

VENICE

McIntyre had been travelling in his boat for what felt like forever. Eventually he saw a light. His eyes adjusted to the approaching glow.

The tunnel finally exited out onto the Grande Canal in Venice. McIntyre guided his boat out onto the busy waterway. Boats of all shapes and sizes travelled here there and everywhere. Delivery barges with heavy loads punted past transporting food to the markets and restaurants.

Reflections from the beautiful, white buildings bordering the canal danced and sparkled in the aquamarine water, and high above terracotta tiled roofs glowed ablaze in the Italian sun.

McIntyre did not have time to enjoy the Italian architecture or cuisine. His focus was on his mission, and he could not afford to screw it up again.

McIntyre found his way to his hotel and berthed his boat. The large entrance of the hotel was formal but inviting. Opulent chandeliers suspended from the ceiling and a grand, sweeping staircase took centre stage in the foyer. He approached the front desk and smiled at the receptionist.

"Ciao, come posso aiutare?" *(Hello, how can I help you?)* greeted the female receptionist.

"Sala dicianove per il signor Horner." *(Room nineteen for Mr Horner.)* McIntyre replied.

The receptionist checked her computer, turned round, and selected a tasselled key from an elaborate pigeon-hole display, then handed a key to McIntyre.

"Buona giornata." *(Have a good day)* she said smiling.

"Grazie." McIntyre replied.

McIntyre left the reception and made his way to his room. On reaching the door to room nineteen, he put the key in the lock and opened it.

"Afternoon McIntyre." said a figure in the corner of the dark room.

Taken by surprise McIntyre swore under his breath then asked, "Who the hell are you?"

McIntyre turned on the light and walked over to the man.

"My name is agent Henderson." answered the man.

McIntyre studied Henderson closely. He did not appear to be a threat, nevertheless McIntyre was not taking any chances. McIntyre quickly drew out his gun and pointed it at Henderson.

"You can put that away. I'm here to assist you. Now, agent McIntyre …" said Henderson.

McIntyre interrupted him, "I am not an agent! I am an assassin, and I know why you're here. You're just a bloody supervisor!" he said angrily through clenched teeth.

Henderson shifted in his seat nervously as McIntyre got closer to his face.

McIntyre stared hard at Henderson, then impatiently asked, "Well! Are you going to tell me what the mission is about then?"

"Right … erm yes." said Henderson taking a deep breath.

Fumbling at the locks on his briefcase Henderson eventually opened it to reveal a small projector inside. He pressed a button on the projector and a beam of light appeared on the wall in front of them. McIntyre walked back to the door and switched off the light.

Flickering black and white images from an archived film transmitted from the projector and appeared the wall.

Henderson cleared his throat then went on to explain. "In 1945 the Japanese surrendered to the Americans as World War Two came to an end. The Americans ordered the Japanese to hand over their bombs which they reluctantly complied with. The Americans transported the bombs to Washington DC then in an attempt to make them untraceable scratched all Japanese identification markings off them.

As you know during the Cold War the British government negotiated a deal with the Americans and allowed them to place a nuclear naval base off the Scottish coast as a deterrent from any possible Soviet Nuclear attack on the UK and the West.

At the same time, another stock of smaller bombs was covertly acquired by the British government. They were hidden in the UK in a different location under the code name 'Operation Bleeding Red Gate'. These were the Japanese bombs with the identification markings scratched off, so when the British acquired them, they were unaware of their original source.

Over a period of time the location of the bombs became buried in files and paperwork. Also, those responsible for obtaining them had passed away, and so the existence of the bombs was unknown and their location remained hidden.

From our undercover agents and reliable sources in the criminal world, information began to filter through about a quest to find an ancient sword."

"What has a sword to do with the bombs?" asked McIntyre interrupting Henderson.

"I'm just coming to that." Henderson explained. He cleared his throat again and continued. "Before the Japanese handed the bombs over in 1945 to the Americans, they secretly installed tracking devises inside each one. The Japanese were eventually able to locate the bombs and the coordinates were recorded and concealed inside an ancient relic called the Komodo Katana, a unique Japanese sword.

However, this too was lost through time. Since then, many people have searched for the sword but were unsuccessful, until now. That is why we are here in Venice McIntyre. Tomorrow the sword is up for sale at Sotheby's Auction House."

"Great, let's pick it up then." said McIntyre.

"Ah." replied Henderson smiling. "It's not as simple as that." he sighed, then continued to explain.

"There are several known thieves and terrorists searching for the sword. One of those is Sebastian Dubois, a master thief, who is planning to steal it for his own private collection. The sword, after all, is an ancient relic and priceless. Dubois is not aware of its internal secret or how it came to be lost. However, he is not our biggest problem."

McIntyre curious as to what Henderson was about to say turned to face him.

"An old Japanese veteran has also tracked the sword down. He goes by the name of The Shogun. Although he is old and frail, he is a very powerful and dangerous man. We need to keep it out of The Shogun's hands at all costs. He knows what the sword contains and will stop at nothing to get it." explained Henderson.

Henderson paused for a moment. His mouth was dry from talking. He poured a glass of water then quickly gulped down the whole glass. Wiping his lips with the back of his hand, he turned to McIntyre and continued his briefing.

"I hope you understand the enormity of this mission McIntyre. We are dealing with the possibility of a nuclear war or World War Three. The consequences of not stopping The Shogun could be catastrophic. Tonight, you and I will be attending a party at the Rialto Club. There will be another assassin named Raoul Alverez at the party. He plans to meet with Dubois and assist him with stealing the sword. We dispose of Alverez, you take on his identity, meet with Dubois and use him to get the Komodo Katana." said Henderson finishing his instructions.

"Simple as that then." replied McIntyre sarcastically.

Henderson closed his briefcase and turned to McIntyre again. "I'll see you later then." he said nervously and hurried out of the room.

....

That night McIntyre and Henderson attended The Rialto Club in the northern district of Venice.

They passed through the grand entrance and walked into the main dance hall.

Deafening, heavy music pulsated, and throbbed, and blue and white beams of light flashed to the beat while a mass of bodies jumped up and down on the dance floor.

"McIntyre!!" yelled Henderson over the music "I've located Dubois!!"

Henderson pointed to a tall blonde man leaning against the bar surrounded by bodyguards. Dubois did not fit the typical stereotype of a thief. He looked wealthy and was wearing an expensive sky-blue tailored suit.

"We need to find Alverez first!" McIntyre shouted back.

McIntyre reached in his pocket and took out the DNA tracking devices he had been given by Woods.

"These are DNA scanners! They should be able to pinpoint Alverez. The more vibration you get the closer you're getting to him!" shouted McIntyre.

McIntyre and Henderson moved around the dancefloor. The only vibration they detected was the heavy beat from the club music. It buzzed through every fibre of their body.

They moved to the back of the dance hall. McIntyre then lifted the device up and felt it vibrate in his hand.

"He's up the stairs!" yelled McIntyre.

"How are we going to get up there?!" Henderson asked.

McIntyre reached into his pocket again and pulled out two VIP passes. Surprised at McIntyre's astuteness Henderson took the pass from McIntyre and smiled. They found the main stairwell, presented their passes, and went upstairs.

McIntyre tested the scanner again. The display showed that Alverez was up another level.

Henderson and McIntyre walked towards a balcony overlooking the dance floor. They looked up the internal atrium and saw the club had several floors. On the top floor were private suites and a dining room.

"We need to get up there!" McIntyre said to Henderson.

"How? They have security checking everyone entering the area. Even with the VIP passes were going to get searched. Not only will they remove our guns, but they're likely to shoot us with them." replied Henderson.

McIntyre looked around for an alternative route. "This way." he said and walked over to an open window. Then quickly he stepped out on to a narrow ledge.

McIntyre looked to his right and saw an external fire staircase leading up to a small balcony on the top floor. He swung himself off the ledge, onto the metal staircase then made his way up the stairs. Henderson followed behind him.

On reaching the balcony McIntyre climbed over a metal railing then paused to neaten his jacket. He stretched his hand out to help Henderson over the railing.

Waiting for Henderson to compose himself, McIntyre checked the DNA tracker again and pinpointed Alverez's position.

"Ready?" asked McIntyre. Henderson nodded back to him.

From the balcony McIntyre and Henderson walked through open glazed doors and entered a vast dining room. A large number of VIP guests were being wined and dined at an extravagant dinner and there was a loud chatter of voices. Walking quickly through the tables nobody questioned their presence.

On leaving the dining room they entered a circular hallway at the top of the atrium. Lifeless bodies of several security staff lay scattered in the hallway. It was obvious Alverez had been here moments before and left a trail of destruction in his wake.

"Why is he attacking the Security? I thought he was here to meet Dubois?" asked Henderson.

McIntyre shrugged his shoulders but had a feeling Alverez was here for another reason.

Ahead was a door with a sign on it. The sign read 'Privato! Nessun Accesso Consentito' (*Private! No Access Allowed*). The door was slightly ajar. McIntyre and Henderson cautiously entered through the door and up into the attic.

It was dark and dusty in the eaves of the attic. Wooden planks beneath their feet creaked as they carefully stepped further in. The heavy bass music from the club below covered the sound of their movements.

Henderson then saw Alverez stepping onto a metal platform with a large crowbar in his hand. He signalled silently to McIntyre and pointed towards Alverez.

On the metal platform Alverez stood beside a winch. The winch was holding up a huge chandelier which was directly above the bar and dance floor of the Rialto Night Club.

McIntyre's instincts were correct. Alverez was not planning to meet Dubois. He was planning to kill him.

Alverez lifted the crowbar up over his head then brought it down hard onto the winch. There was a loud clang. He raised his arms again repeating his actions.

Henderson aimed his gun at Alverez and fired but missed. The heavy bass music from the club below muffled the sound of the gunshot but Alverez saw the sparks from the bullet as it ricocheted off the metal platform. He quickly turned around.

McIntyre leapt towards Alverez and grabbed him by the throat. Alverez, a huge powerful man, took McIntyre's leg and with ease flipped him over, slamming McIntyre onto his back on the platform.

McIntyre groaned as he hit the hard metal surface. Alverez then grabbed McIntyre and hurled him off the platform.

Alverez picked up the crowbar and was just about to hit the winch again when suddenly sparks appeared on the crowbar and it flew out of his hands.

Henderson had aimed correctly this time and seemed quite pleased with himself, but his happiness was short lived. His eyes widened as he saw Alverez draw out his Glock Pistol and point it directly at him.

The music from the club suddenly stopped. There was a short pause as Alverez hesitated to shoot.

"ARE YOU REAAAAAADYYYY!!!!!" yelled the DJ, then the heavy beat of the club music began again. Alverez and Henderson started shooting at each other. Each shot seemed to coincide with the beat of the music.

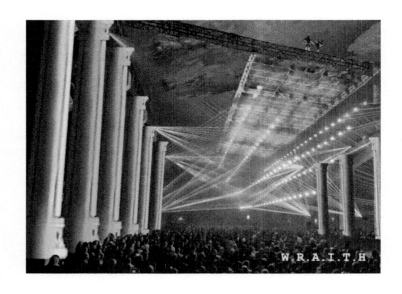

McIntyre quickly stood up and launched himself at Alverez again. He wrestled with the Glock in Alverez hands. Alverez eventually lost grip and the gun soared through the air, landing at the far end of the attic.

McIntyre attempted to kick Alverez in the chest, but his kick only moved Alverez an inch backwards. Alverez grinned then returned a kick into McIntyre's chest, the force of which catapulted McIntyre to the edge of the platform.

Alverez picked up the crowbar and pulled it back over his head. He was about to bring it down on to McIntyre when two loud gun shots rang out.

Alverez's huge body then crashed down on the platform. McIntyre turned around and saw Henderson with his gun still pointed forward at Alverez.

"Good shot." said McIntyre dragging himself up.

McIntyre picked up Alverez's phone, looked down at the screen and read the last message which was still open.

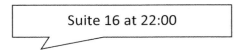

Suite 16 at 22:00

"Go back to the hotel now. I'll meet you back there after my meeting with Dubois." McIntyre said to Henderson.

"Stay on coms." replied Henderson as he left the attic.

McIntyre walked over to the other side of the attic and picked up the Glock. He returned to Alverez who lay face down on the floor and gave him a prod with his foot. He then stepped over the lifeless body and walked out of the attic.

The music from the club was still beating away and the dancers continued to writhe about. Dubois and his bodyguards watched on from the bar, relaxed and happily consuming their drinks, unaware that their lives had ever been in danger.

CHAPTER SIX

SUITE 16

So as not to alert Dubois's men McIntyre hid the bodies of the security staff which lay in the hallway. He then made his way through the upper floors of the club to Dubois's private suite.

Two muscular bodyguards stood at the double doors of Suite 16. McIntyre introduced himself as Alverez, then the bodyguards opened the doors.

McIntyre walked into a vestibule. A butler approached McIntyre holding up a silver plate. Without the butler having to speak McIntyre knew what he was required to do and placed Alverez's Glock pistol down on it. The butler then guided McIntyre through to a large spacious room.

If front of him sat Dubois relaxing on a red velvet chaise longue. He looked up as McIntyre entered the room.

"Mr Alverez is here to see you Sir," said the butler introducing McIntyre to Dubois and he quietly left the room.

"So, Alverez is an alias. Am I right? Because you don't look very Spanish to me." said Dubois looking at McIntyre's pale Scottish skin.

"You could say so." replied McIntyre.

Dubois stood up and walked over to McIntyre. He studied McIntyre's clothes judgementally which were crumpled and dusty from his fight with Alverez in the attic.

"A drink?" proposed Dubois.

"No thank you." McIntyre replied.

"Ah, I see, you're a man of getting down to the business." said Dubois.

Dubois clicked his fingers. The butler returned carrying a rolled-up blueprint and placed it on a table then left the room once more.

McIntyre held one end of the blueprint and Dubois the other, together they unravelled and stretched it out over the table.

"I want this sword Alverez. I don't want this raid to be a cockup. So, listen carefully, this is what I want you to do" said Dubois, he then gave McIntyre a set of instructions to follow.

"If you betray me Alverez, I won't order one of my men to kill you. I shall do it myself." said Dubois coldly.

Dubois forced a smile at McIntyre then let go of the blueprint.

"Be on time." said Dubois. "And …" he paused to look at McIntyre, "Get yourself some better clothes." he said arrogantly.

McIntyre, tempted as he was to make some cheeky remark, did not reply. He picked up the blueprint, retrieved the Glock then left the suite and made his way down the stairs.

Dubois calmly walked out of his suite into the atrium. He watched McIntyre closely as he made his way down the stairs towards the dance floor.

Pushing his way through the throng of clubbers, McIntyre eventually reached the front door and exited the building.

Dubois returned to his suite.

"Faut-il le suivre?" (*Should we follow him?*) one of Dubois's bodyguards asked.

"Non, je sais quoi faire." (*No, I know what to do*) Dubois replied.

CHAPTER SEVEN

VENICE AUCTION

The next day the sun was shining bright on the city of Venice. Couples happily passed their time in gondolas up and down the canal, while others hurried from stall to stall buying food from the market. All seemed as it should be.

In the district of San Marco an elderly Asian man sat quietly in Sotheby's Auction House. He was of small stature and his skin was wrinkled and mottled with old age.

Standing close by him was his bodyguard. The bodyguard's eyes shifted around the room, suspicious of everyone attending the auction.

The old man rhythmically tapped his fingers on his walking stick. He removed a gold pocket watch from his jacket, stared at the slow ticking hands on the timepiece then snapped it shut.

This frail looking old man was The Shogun, and he had come to reclaim the Katana.

....

At the same time a small motorboat carrying the Katana sword headed towards the auction along the Grande Canal accompanied by a police escort.

By the banks of the canal Dubois and two of his henchmen sat quietly. They watched the boats closely as they made their way to the auction House. Dubois discreetly held up a small silver baton, aimed it at the boats and pressed a button. Electromagnetic pellets rapidly fired from the baton which then attached to the underside of the boats.

Unaware of the pellets the motorboat and Police escort continued calmly on down the canal. The boats then turned into a narrow rio waterway. They had no idea they were falling into Dubois's trap.

Further down the canal McIntyre along with Dubois's other henchmen waited patiently in their boats.

McIntyre was wearing the bullet-proof Raven suit Benson had issued him. He wasn't wearing the suit to satisfy Dubois's arrogance; he was wearing it because he anticipated extensive gunfire today and he wasn't taking any chances.

McIntyre put on his leather gloves, while Dubois's henchmen loaded their guns in the buildings beside him.

The motorboat and police escort came into view and entered a side rio waterway where McIntyre and the henchmen were waiting.

McIntyre picked up a remote device.

"Do it now!" shouted one of Dubois's henchmen at McIntyre

McIntyre pressed a button on the devise. Just then the pellets on the underside police escort and motorboat engaged, causing the engines of both boats to suddenly stop.

Dubois's henchmen took aim at the Police. They attempted to shoot but their guns jammed.

"What the hell is this?" yelled one of the henchmen.

McIntyre smiled at him. The henchman looked puzzled, then realised this was McIntyre's doing.

McIntyre pressed a button on another device. An underwater blast created a pressurised eruption of water and flipped the motorboat carrying the sword upside down.

McIntyre quickly opened fire at Dubois's confused henchmen.

…………..

Inside the auction house The Shogun heard the distant gunfire. Instinctively he knew his plan had been ruined.

He cursed under his breath and gestured to his bodyguard to follow him.

"Sorera o sagashi ni ikimasu!" *(Go find them!)* ordered The Shogun.

The bodyguard nodded and left the auction house.

……….

While McIntyre did his best to distract Dubois's men, Henderson, in diving gear, swam underwater towards the upturned boat.

He had to act fast, McIntyre would only be able to hold off Dubois's men for a short time. Fortunately, he knew exactly what he was looking for. He didn't have to look long.

Fixed to the side of the boat was a small crate. Immediately he smashed it open. Inside resting on straw was the Katana sword. He separated the blade and handle and removed a small glass cylinder.

He placed the cylinder in a secure pouch on his wetsuit and discarded the sword, which then sank to the bottom of the canal.

....

McIntyre finally stopped firing and raced off in one of the henchmen's motorboats.

"Suivez-le! Suivez-le!" (*Follow Him! Follow Him!*) shouted one of the henchmen.

Two other boats carrying Dubois's men immediately chased after McIntyre. The remaining men left behind then attacked the Police, seized their boat and guns, and quickly joined in the hunt for McIntyre.

....

With Dubois's men gone Henderson climbed his way out of the water and discarded his mask and air tank. He checked his pocket to make sure he still had the cylinder. This small discreet item contained the co-ordinates of the lost bombs. This was what The Shogun came for and what Henderson must protect at all costs.

Henderson pulled on a crash helmet and straddled a motorbike parked on the fondamenta bank. He turned the ignition on, revved the engine, then made his way back to the hotel.

In an alleyway a figure of a man standing in the shadows watched Henderson from a distance.

CHAPTER EIGHT

VENICE PURSUIT

McIntyre in his motorboat emerged from a side rio waterway onto the Grande Canal. He expertly weaved his way around numerous shuttle boats and other floating obstacles in the water.

Turning sharply, he brought his motorboat alongside a small wooden pier. He jumped off onto the platform then ran up several steps towards the Ponte de Rialto bridge.

On the bridge a large number of tourists quietly meandered through the arcade of shops. Large groups of sightseers posed for photos, trying to create the perfect backdrop for their next online post.

McIntyre merge into the crowd and made his way up the steps to the middle of the bridge.

All a sudden there was a loud burst of automatic gunfire. Tourists started screaming and quickly ran for safety, some taking shelter in the small gift shops that spanned the bridge.

Dubois's men appeared in their boats below the bridge and two of the men jumped off onto the pier. They then started to close in on McIntyre.

McIntyre lifted his gun, took aim and pulled the trigger but he was out of bullets.

With tremendous power and perfect aim McIntyre hurled his gun and hit one of the henchmen dead centre on his face. The stunned henchman tripped and fell on the steps. McIntyre ran forward, grabbed the henchman's head, and buried it into a stone balustrade on the bridge.

McIntyre turned round to see another henchman approaching. He threw himself with huge force at the man, then together they both crashed through a gift shop window.

McIntyre and the man continued to fight on the shop floor, sprawling through shards of glass and broken display fittings. McIntyre grabbed a metal shelf, swung round, and struck the henchman on the side of his neck. The henchman's knees buckled then he fell heavily onto the shop floor.

McIntyre scrambled his way out of the broken shop window and ran to the other side of the bridge. Another large henchman stood blocking his path.

McIntyre sized the man up then continued to run towards him. He picked up speed then launched himself in the air, spun his body round and hook kicked the henchman in the head, causing the man to lose his balance and fall into the canal below.

McIntyre grabbed the henchman's abandoned gun which lay on the ground. He stood up quickly and saw one of Dubois's motorboats moving under the bridge.

McIntyre jumped over the bridge balustrade onto the boat below. The henchmen on the boat were taken by surprise. McIntyre easily fought them off and threw them both overboard. He quickly took control of the vessel and veered off into the narrow rio canals of San Marco.

By now Dubois had received word of McIntyre's betrayal and he was also hunting him down. He was not going to let McIntyre get away with this.

Dubois's men waiting in motorboats on the other side of the bridge spotted McIntyre, opened fire, and began to give chase.

Twisting and turning at high speed they ripped their motorboats through the narrow waterways. Bullets ricocheted off balconies and railings. The noise of gunfire was immense as it amplified off the buildings that surrounded them.

Ahead of McIntyre, emerging from another rio canal, a small delivery boat was slowly entering his path. McIntyre swerved abruptly, and narrowly missed it.

He looked back at Dubois's men. There was an almighty crash as their motorboat ran straight through the centre of the delivery boat. The wooden body of the delivery boat shattered into a million pieces and its contents, including the driver, were catapulted through the air. Despite this, the henchmen kept coming.

McIntyre found himself slowing down, having to navigate his way through the maze of narrow rio canals crammed with long delivery barges. He turned round to see Dubois's men closing in on him.

Gradually the rio canal became less congested and McIntyre once again increased his speed. He revved up a gear and ducked his head as he passed under several low bridges.

Eventually he reached a brilliant white building, then exited out of the rio canal onto the enormous Bacino San Marco lagoon.

Various shapes and sizes of boats swamped the busy lagoon. Vaporetto bus-boats taxied up and down, private yachts chartered through the bay and a multitude of small gondolas carrying couples rowed steadily through the water.

McIntyre swerved his motorboat to avoid colliding with a gondola. Turning the steering wheel sharp left he then guided his motorboat to the side of a large bus-boat.

Following close behind, Dubois's henchmen entered the lagoon. They loaded their guns and sat waiting for McIntyre to appear round the other side of the bus-boat.

Suddenly McIntyre emerged at full speed toward Dubois's men. It looked like he was going for a head on collision. At the last moment McIntyre swerved his motorboat clipping the hull of one of the henchmen's boats which then started spinning rapidly. There was a loud blast as the spinning boat struck another boat and exploded into flames.

McIntyre turned his motorboat around and quickly sped off up the lagoon. He reached a large cruise terminal and turned his boat back into Venice through the narrow rio canals.

Turning around a tight bend McIntyre brought his boat up to a siding and jump off onto a fondamenta bank.

Running down the bank McIntyre then disappeared into a dark passage.

Dubois's henchmen continued to follow McIntyre. They thought they had lost him but soon spied his abandoned motorboat.

The henchmen pulled over to the side and jumped onto the bank. On the ground they spotted McIntyre's wet footprints. One of the henchmen signalled silently to the rest of the men to follow him.

Running through the narrow streets of the city, McIntyre tried to shake off Dubois's men. The maze of streets became narrower and more complexed. It would be easy to get completely lost in here thought McIntyre to himself.

McIntyre entered another street which was a dead end. He stepped back and hid in the dark shadows.

Dubois's men ran past, not knowing where McIntyre had gone, they kept searching.

McIntyre could hear the faint yelling of the police. He came out from hiding and turned in the opposite direction of Dubois's men.

Suddenly, out of nowhere Dubois appeared. He knocked McIntyre's gun out of his hand and pushed him against a wall in the alleyway.

"I'm a man of my word! Now you are a dead man!" he growled at McIntyre.

A furious fight erupted between Dubois and McIntyre. Both men repeatedly punched and kicked each other.

Dubois reached inside his jacket pocket, then in a fast-sweeping motion withdrew his hand and exposed a knife.

McIntyre jumped back and kept his eyes focused on the blade. Dubois moved forward waving the knife in frenzied strikes. McIntyre suddenly grabbed Dubois's hand and managed to seize the knife. With the knife now in his possession, McIntyre moved forward to attack Dubois.

In the dark street, flashes of light reflected off the blade as the men carried on their violent struggle.

Dubois seized McIntyre's arm and swung him around out of the narrow street and onto a fondamenta bank.

McIntyre lost his footing and fell heavily onto his back. The knife dropped out of his hand, and he lay motionless on the ground.

Dubois saw the knife and quickly picked it up. He knelt over McIntyre and raised the knife above his head.

"Remember, I told you, if you betray me, I will kill you myself!" sneered Dubois.

There was a loud crack from a single gunshot being fired.

Blood splattered all over McIntyre's face. Dubois stared blankly at McIntyre. He slumped forward, then his lifeless body fell to the ground.

McIntyre scrambled to his feet and stared in the direction of the gunfire.

Squinting his eyes McIntyre saw a woman standing in the shadows. She was smartly dressed, and he recognized her pale face.

"Emma?" asked McIntyre, puzzled as to why his sister stood in front of him.

"Hello Fergus." she replied.

They approached each other.

"Why are you here?" asked McIntyre.

"NCA business." answered Emma.

In the distance a voice shouted, "Officer McIntyre!"

Emma and McIntyre both turned to face the direction of the voice.

"It's me they're calling for." said Emma. "Go! Now!" she said pleading with her brother.

McIntyre quickly retrieved his gun then sped off into the maze of streets. A squad of officers approached Emma.

"What the hell is this?" asked Emma's superior officer enraged and looking down at Dubois's dead body.

"I had to shoot. He was terrorising civilians." answered Emma.

Furious by her obvious coverup to protect her brother, the superior officer yelled at her, "Clean up this mess and find your idiot brother!"

. . . .

A short time later McIntyre arrived at his hotel. He made his way to his room and opened the door to find Henderson there.

"Did you get it?" asked McIntyre.

"Yes" said Henderson walking over to the window.

Suddenly, there was rapid gunfire. Shards of glass sprayed all over the hotel room from the window and Henderson collapsed to the floor.

Henderson held his hand up to his chest as blood seeped through his crisp, white shirt. He looked over at McIntyre in shock then collapsed on the floor.

The gunfire continued, perforating the hotel room with bullet holes. McIntyre ducked down and took cover below the window frame. He could hear the direction of the gunfire but could not see who was shooting at them.

McIntyre looked around the room then grabbed a small bedside mirror. Slowly lifting the mirror up over the window frame, he located the gunman in the reflection.

Skilfully McIntyre tilted the mirror and twisted it towards the sky. The reflection of the sun bounced off the glass and threw back a beam of light in the direction of the gunfire. The flash of light was so strong it blinded the gunman.

While the gunman struggled to see, McIntyre took this opportunity to find the co-ordinates. He searched in Henderson's pockets and found the cylinder.

McIntyre took the small tube and placed it carefully into his own jacket. He then checked Henderson for a pulse but could not find one.

McIntyre did not have time to waste, he needed to get out of there.

Grabbing Henderson's briefcase, he escaped from the room and quickly left the hotel.

. . . .

That evening McIntyre boarded a train at Santa Lucia station in Venice. His plan was to head for the nearest airport and get back to London.

Just then McIntyre received an anonymous call on his mobile.

"Hello Mr McIntyre." a frail, male voice said with an Asian accent.

"Who is this? How did you get this number?" McIntyre asked.

"Let's just say I am a powerful man." the voice replied.

"The Shogun." guessed McIntyre.

"Hmm, I guess you have heard of me. I've heard of you too McIntyre and understand that you are quite a man to be reckoned with. I also know that you have stolen something of mine." said The Shogun.

"Stolen? Ah, you mean the Katana. If you want it, you can find it at the bottom of the canal." said McIntyre mockingly.

"No! Mr McIntyre you know what I want!" snapped The Shogun getting impatient.

"If you mean the co-ordinates, they never belonged to you." replied McIntyre.

"Ah, ah, ah! Careful now." warned The Shogun. "Words can be tools for death. They can also be tools for sparing souls. Now listen, I want you to meet me in Singapore on the roof of the Marina Bay Sands Hotel. We can …"

The Shogun paused for a moment to find the right word then he continued. "Negotiate, yes, over the co-ordinates then your life may be spared. I hope you make the right decision. Goodbye Mr McIntyre." The Shogun finished speaking and ended the phone call.

The train suddenly jolted as it slowly departed the station. McIntyre put down his phone on an adjacent seat then opened Henderson's briefcase a took out the laptop.

Using an encrypted search McIntyre tried to find out some more information about The Shogun. There wasn't much, although there was evidence showing he was connected to several criminal organisations.

McIntyre did some more searching and found an old associate of The Shogun located on an island in Indonesia.

McIntyre decided to change his journey back to London. He needed to know more about The Shogun. More importantly, he needed to know how to stop him.

CHAPTER NINE

INDONESIA

After several connecting flights and numerous taxis', McIntyre finally reached his destination on Singkep island. He walked along a deserted beach towards a dilapidated wooden house.

McIntyre knocked on the door. An elderly, Asian man appeared at the door. He held up a shotgun and pointed it straight between McIntyre's eyes.

"Who are you? What do you want?" he asked aggressively.

"I'm Fergus McIntyre." explained McIntyre. "I need some information about The Shogun."

The man shut the door hard in McIntyre's face, but McIntyre wedged his foot in the doorway stopping it from closing.

"I'm trying to stop him." said McIntyre pushing the door open again.

The old man stared hard at McIntyre, then lowered his gun. "Fine, come in then." he said reluctantly.

Resting his shotgun against a wall the old man then grabbed hold of a stick to steady himself and shuffled to the other side of the room. Although the man was clearly not wealthy, he kept his home neat and tidy and everything had its place. Eventually he sat down and started to talk.

"Yes, I know The Shogun." said the old man. "We worked together a long time ago. I want no part in what he has done or is doing now. I came here to get away from all the war and death, to live a quiet life." he said with his voice shaking with a combination old age and trepidation.

McIntyre explained to the old man how he knew of him already and his association with The Shogun. "Yes Yuki, I know who you are. But I'm not here to cause you any trouble." He said trying to reassure the old man.

The old man looked surprised when McIntyre used his name.

"The Shogun has asked me to meet him in Singapore. I need your help. Tell me all you know about him." asked McIntyre.

Yuki sighed and took a deep breath. Recalling old memories about The Shogun was something he tried to avoid, but he could tell McIntyre needed his help.

"His real name is Asahi. We were both young men then, just teenagers. We worked at Riken alongside scientists in a nuclear research laboratory during World War Two. Asahi was difficult to work with. You kept out of his way when he got angry. I was his second assistant; he killed his first." explained Yuki shaking his head.

"In the spring of 1945 the American's bombed our laboratory. We salvaged what we could and relocated. Then in the summer they dropped the atomic bombs on Hiroshima and Nagasaki." Yuki's eyes filled with tears. His face contorted as he remembered the devastation the bombings caused.

With his voice wavering Yuki tried to continue. "Later that same year the War came to an end. I remember it well. We had just finished our lunch, when I received a phone call to inform us that Japan had surrendered. I sent a someone to go break the news to Asahi. Then I heard gunshots. He shot the messenger at close range. Asahi didn't have to do that; the messenger was only a boy!" said Yuki angrily.

Yuki leaned over and offered McIntyre some tea.

"No thank you." said McIntyre politely. "What became of Asahi after the war?"

Yuki poured himself a cup of tea and sat back on his makeshift wooden chair.

"After the war the Americans launched 'Operation Paperclip'. It was a secret intelligence operation where the Americans recruited adversary expert scientists and engineers from Germany and Japan to work for the American government. The idea was that the experts would assist the Americans during the Cold War making chemical bombs and rockets for them. Although we were only laboratory assistants, they wanted to recruit us too. Asahi was insulted and refused to comply. He considered working for the Russians who had a similar campaign, but Asahi wanted to be his own leader. He then went into hiding and was involved in several underground radical groups. Over the years Asahi set up a militant group named 'Adauchi', which means vengeance in Japanese. The group grew and grew. Today the Adauchi is a worldwide terrorist organisation." explained Yuki.

Yuki lifted his cup and sipped some more tea, then cleared his throat and continued to disclose all he knew to McIntyre. "Asahi wants the Japanese bombs back that the Americans took. He needs the co-ordinates to find them.

I'm not sure what he plans to do with the bombs, but I can guess if he gets hold of them, then he will seek revenge." said Yuki.

Trying to get a better understanding of The Shogun, McIntyre continued to quiz Yuki and they talked late into the evening.

Yuki slowly stood up and came closer to McIntyre. "Be careful Fergus. He only wants you there in Singapore to control you. He might even try to recruit you. Do not be fooled by his appearance, he may look frail, but he is a very powerful man. Singapore is his domain, and he has lots of allies there. If you go, he won't negotiate with you, he'll just kill you." said Yuki cautioning McIntyre.

"I have to try." McIntyre replied. He stood up and thanked Yuki then walked out of the house onto the beach.

McIntyre stared at the sun setting over the South China Sea. The glowing fire ball gradually receded into the cool waters then disappeared below the horizon. He paused for a moment, he now had a better understanding of The Shogun and knew what had to be done.

CHAPTER TEN

SINGAPORE

A star filled night sky wrapped its velvet blanket over the vast city of Singapore.

On the rooftop of the Marina Bay Sands Hotel, McIntyre stood quietly drinking a cocktail at a bar next to the swimming pool.

He looked out over the majestic skyline. Billions of multi-coloured neon lights spread out over the city, multiplying themselves as watery reflections in the Marina Bay.

McIntyre's phone vibrated ending the peaceful setting. It was a text from Emma.

We need to talk. I'm in the garden

McIntyre finished his drink then left the bar. He took the elevator down to the hotel lobby and walked out of the building towards the gardens in front of the hotel.

A network of winding paths led him through the radiant gardens which were covered in a spectrum of ever-changing neon lights.

McIntyre made his way towards the enormous illuminated artificial trees in the centre of the garden. At the base of one tree, he saw Emma sitting alone.

"Hello Fergus." said Emma.

"Why are you here?" asked McIntyre brashly.

"Nice to see you too Fergus." Emma replied.

"I said, why are you here?" snapped McIntyre.

"Several special force units around the world have voiced their displeasure and concerns about you. I have been sent to inform you that you and your team at M.I.5 need to stand down from this operation and let us at the NCA take over." explained Emma.

"So, you're telling me to back off!" said McIntyre sharply.

"If you don't Fergus, someone might just take you out to make their plans easier. I don't want to see my brother die. I'm here to reason with you." explained Emma.

"I know a damn sight more than you and your NCA will ever know!" McIntyre shouted furiously.

"Do you think I came all this way to ask you Fergus! I'm not asking you! I'm ordering you on behalf of our government. We all know you're one of the most elite M.I.5 assassins, that you have a special code name 'The Wraith' - but for fudge sake Fergus by being a maverick you're going down a road where you'll be seen as a traitor to our country and our allies!" said Emma frustratedly.

McIntyre laughed at her. Emma gave her brother a hard stare before going red in the face.

"Is that you trying to swear Emma? Fudge Sake. Ha, you always were a goody-two-shoes and always trying to do the right thing. Look, I don't take orders from you and just because you're my sister doesn't mean I'm going to listen. You're not going to change my mind." said McIntyre defiantly.

There was a pause in their conversation. Family was not something they talked about easily and their thoughts drifted to their unusual childhood.

McIntyre quickly resumed the conversation. He was incensed by the audacity of his sister and the NCA asking him to step aside. He gritted his teeth and faced his sister.

"Look! I've been given this mission. I'm going to see it through and I'm going to stop The Shogun whether you, the NCA or anyone else likes it or not!" shouted McIntyre then he started to walk away from his sister.

One of Emma's colleagues approached McIntyre and tried to reason with him. "Sir, I'd strongly advice you not to do tha.,.aarggh!" he groaned as McIntyre punched him in the stomach.

Undercover NCA officers dotted around the garden revealed themselves and aimed their weapons at McIntyre.

"STAND DOWN!!!!" yelled Emma.

McIntyre kept moving then quickly ran off back to the hotel.

"Damn it." said Emma angrily as she flopped back down on her seat under the illuminated tree.

....

In the undergrowth of the garden a man lay hidden out of sight. He had recorded the entire conversation between Emma & McIntyre on his phone. He lifted his phone to his ear.

"Sir, did you get all of that?" the man asked.

"Yes. Yes, I did." a familiar voice said on the other end of the phone.

"Terminate the deal that I had with Mr McIntyre. Retire his life" continued the voice, then the man hung up.

. . . .

The next day, McIntyre woke in his hotel suite. He had rested well, but he was troubled by what his sister had said the day before. Maybe he should back down he thought to himself.

He sat up slowly, swung his feet out of his bed and onto the cold floor. Standing up he walked towards the chair where his clothes were neatly folded and got dressed.

McIntyre walked through his hotel suite to a small kitchen area and poured himself a coffee. He made his way over to a table near the window and sat down.

From his hotel suite on the fifty first floor the view was breath-taking but quite different from the previous evening. The neon landscape was transformed into a lush green garden, verged with industrial buildings and modern architecture.

His thoughts turned once more to his sister. She didn't have all the facts and why was the government wanting to stop him? To get this job done I'm going to have to stop The Shogun myself he deliberated. His frustration and bewilderment began to make him angry.

"What does she know that I don't?" he said out loud to the empty hotel room. "Emma and the NCA will just mess this up. I'm not giving up on my mission." he said firmly.

Irritated by his sister's interventions he swung round on his chair and opened his laptop, clicked on a mapping system, and typed in the bomb co-ordinates: 55.951907, -3.189636

McIntyre watched the screen on his laptop as the system calculated the numbers. Suddenly a red arrow appeared pointing over a map.

McIntyre looked at the screen and frowned. He checked the co-ordinates again. Surely this can't be right he thought as he stared puzzling at the map on the screen.

The arrow was pointing directly over Waverley Train Station in Edinburgh. Not only had the allies betrayed the UK government but they had betrayed his own birthplace he thought to himself.

He felt so angry, then remembered what Adebayo said to him in Brazil.

"If I tell you. You'll turn to our side." McIntyre muttered to himself recalling Adebayo' words.

Finding this difficult to believe he looked down again at the laptop. In the reflection of the screen, he saw a dark figure moving behind him.

McIntyre turned around quickly and saw a man in black, rappelling outside his hotel window onto the balcony.

Within seconds the man had smashed through the window and grabbed McIntyre. Together they went headfirst over the table and onto the floor.

Jumping to his feet the man then reached with his right hand to a sheath on his left hip. A distinctive sound vibrated in the air of metal rubbing on metal as the man drew out a Tantō sword. The man then let out a loud high pitched shrill and ran at speed towards McIntyre.

McIntyre quickly moved out the way as the man brought the blade down over his head.

McIntyre's eyes widened as the sword narrowly missed him, hit the chair he had been sitting on earlier and split it in two.

The man came at McIntyre again this time with short jabs. McIntyre danced around the blade which was coming at him from all angles.

The man grinned as he came closer and closer to McIntyre. The blade of the sword whistled as it cut through the air. McIntyre moved back towards the bedroom.

Suddenly the sword hit a door frame and slipped out the man's hand, it soared across the room then wedged itself into the floor.

Seizing his chance McIntyre pushed the man to the floor, ran to the kitchen area and took cover behind the breakfast bar. He pulled one of the kitchen drawers open, rummaged around in the drawer and found his gun. He stood up and took aim at his attacker but then realised the man had disappeared.

McIntyre walked cautiously through the hotel suite. It was as if the man had vanished into thin air.

Then out of nowhere the man ambushed McIntyre and tackled him to the ground. In doing so he knocked McIntyre's gun out of his hand which then slid across the floor and disappeared under a cabinet.

McIntyre scrambled to his feet and ran towards the door to escape, however his attacker leapt across the room and fought McIntyre to the ground once more.

While McIntyre lay on the floor the attacker scanned the room quickly with his eyes. Finding what he was looking for he reached down to retrieve the Tantō sword. He pulled the sword out of the floor, turned around, and took a swipe at McIntyre.

McIntyre skilfully dodged the blade then grabbed the man's arm. Within seconds he claimed ownership of the sword. He spun round slashing the man's shoulder and neck in the process. Blood projected across the room and onto the walls.

There was a deafening silence as the attacker's limp body suddenly fell to the floor.

McIntyre, exhausted, dropped the Tantō sword and slowly walked to the table where the laptop still lay open. He still couldn't believe the picture on screen was the location of the bombs. What was his government thinking by placing them there?

McIntyre picked up the co-ordinates, put on his jacket and headed for the door. He stopped to look at his dead attacker. On the man's shoulder McIntyre noticed some Japanese characters embroidered on his clothing. It was The Shoguns militant group 'Adauchi'. He stepped over the body and left his trashed hotel suite.

As he entered the hotel corridor McIntyre saw two large men at the end of the passage staring intently at him. He looked towards the other end of the corridor and saw two more. He suspected these men worked for The Shogun.

McIntyre sighed and shook his head.

"When will you give up?" asked McIntyre.

McIntyre reached for his gun but then remembered it slid under a cabinet in his hotel suite. The men approached McIntyre and began to fight.

Skilfully McIntyre fought them off. One of the men then produced a gun. McIntyre quickly wrestled the gun out of the man's hands and used it to shoot two of his attackers.

The remaining men charged at McIntyre, ramming him into the corridor wall. The gun, still in McIntyre's possession, went off firing several stray bullets down the corridor and into the ceiling until it eventually dropped out of McIntyre's hand onto the floor.

One of the men grabbed McIntyre and he felt his body being lifted. Then with one swift movement, the man hurled McIntyre through a doorway into another hotel suite.

Pulling himself back up to his feet McIntyre saw a glint of steel. One of his attackers held a combat knife. The man grinned menacingly at McIntyre, and he lunged forward trying to stab him.

Raising his forearms McIntyre used his martial arts skills to defend himself and block the knife. There was a flurry of hands then the knife flew out of the man's grip and landed across the room.

McIntyre's attackers were large men, they were sweating and showing signs of exhaustion. The more they fought the less agile they became, making themselves easier targets.

McIntyre found the combat knife lying on the floor. He plunged it into the chest of one of his attackers then quickly withdrew it and hurled it at the other.

McIntyre's aim was not perfect, but the knife struck the man in his leg, causing him to scream out in pain.

The man's face contorted as he pulled the knife slowly out of his leg.

There was a second of silence between McIntyre and his remaining attacker. Their eyes locked on each other.

McIntyre then glanced over the man's shoulder at the window behind.

"Nice view you get from up here, don't you think?" McIntyre asked.

To the man's surprise McIntyre ran straight at him. McIntyre then launched himself into the air and kicked the man in his chest with such velocity that he forced the man through the window. The hotel window shattered into a thousand pieces as both men fell through it.

McIntyre managed to grasp at the broken window frame while his attacker tumbled hundreds of feet to his death.

Clinging to the ledge McIntyre tried not to look down at the huge drop below. He slowly pulled himself up through the window frame and back into the hotel suite.

Sitting on the floor McIntyre panted heavily trying to catch his breath, he stared vacantly through the frame of the smashed window. 'When was this going to end?' he thought to himself.

A warm trickle of blood from a large gash above his eye poured down his face and dripped onto the floor. He lifted his hand to wipe his brow and noticed that shards of glass from the window had pierced his hands.

McIntyre stood up and walked to the bathroom, crunching broken glass below his feet with each step he made.

Placing his cupped hands under the running tap he slowly pulled the sharp shards from his hand and watched his blood flow down the drain. After cleaning his wounds, he wrapped his hand in a towel and walked back into the suite.

Looking at the lifeless body of one of his attackers he saw the same embroidered characters of the 'Adauchi' group on the man's jacket.

McIntyre walked back out to the corridor, returned to his room to retrieve his gun then made his way to the roof.

....

The Shogun was enjoying his lunch in the hotel rooftop restaurant. He licked his fingers contently as he finished off the last of his chilli crab dish.

His chief bodyguard leaned towards him and whispered, "With all due respect Sir. I think you're making a mistake."

The Shogun looked up at his bodyguard while chewing the last of his meal.

"What would make you say that?" asked The Shogun calmly while dabbing the corner of his mouth with a cloth napkin.

"Fergus McIntyre is a walking weapon. He never fails. They call him 'The Wraith', the highest standard of an assassin serving his government. He doesn't care who he kills, he has no sympathy or emotion for all the lives he takes, and he does not need a gun to kill you. He is extremely skilled in combat and could kill you with his bare hands in an instant. And you're just sitting here letting him come to you." cautioned the bodyguard.

The Shogun looked at his bodyguard and smiled.

"Do not worry. The Wraith will fall into the net, my boy. He will fall into the net." The Shogun said assuring his bodyguard.

………..

An elevator door opened, and McIntyre stepped out into a corridor full of laundry trolleys. He looked to his right and saw the rooftop swimming pool. He walked to the end of the corridor, pushed open a glass door and went outside.

McIntyre scanned the rooftop and quickly located The Shogun at the restaurant under some red parasols sheltering from the sun. The Shogun made himself conspicuous by surrounding himself with five intimidating bodyguards all dressed in black and wearing sunglasses.

McIntyre made his way over to them. He felt so wound up. His heart was beating fast, and he had a bitter taste in his mouth, as though his heart was pumping sour saliva into his mouth.

McIntyre passed three of The Shogun's bodyguards who did not obstruct him. The remaining two bodyguards stood directly in front of McIntyre. Each one then stepped to the side creating a clear view of The Shogun.

"Ah! Mr McIntyre!" said The Shogun, greeting him insincerely.

"Please." he said continuing to keep up his polite hypocrisy and gestured McIntyre to sit in the seat opposite him.

The chief bodyguard approached McIntyre and put out an open hand gesturing for McIntyre to give him something. McIntyre handed his gun over to him then he sat down facing The Shogun. The two men stared at each other in silence.

Eventually The Shogun spoke.

"My, that's quite a nasty cut you have there." said The Shogun looking at the blood trickly down McIntyre's forehead.

The Shogun raised his hand and a bodyguard offered McIntyre a napkin to wipe the blood. McIntyre reluctantly accepted the napkin and wiped his brow.

"So, McIntyre, you're probably wondering what my weak points are. Let me tell you something, I have no weak points. But I can already see several with you. Perhaps, I give you an example. Well, I know that the NCA is somehow mixed up in all this and they are also trying to find the co-ordinates. Your sister is an operative with them. Yes, am I right?" asked The Shogun.

"Yes." McIntyre replied still wiping the blood off his face.

"My friend over here," The Shogun said pointing to his bodyguard, "says you're some sort of robot, a Wraith. That you have no weak points or no past. However, I know that is not true. Everyone has a past, and it will alv make you weak." said The Shogun smirking.

McIntyre sat quietly listening to The Shogun wondering what he was suggesting. He could hear the faint sound of whirling rotor blades as The Shogun chattered on.

Unexpectedly from the edge of the rooftop pool, a Police helicopter ascended into view.

"Ah, here it is! Your weakest link." said The Shogun laughing and pointing to the helicopter.

"I have my sniper aimed directly at her." explained The Shogun still laughing.

McIntyre took a closer look at the helicopter.

"You've got to be kidding me." said McIntyre shaking his head while looking at Emma in the cockpit of the helicopter.

McIntyre turned to The Shogun. "OK, what do you want me to do?" he shouted at The Shogun trying to be heard over the noise of the helicopter.

"You have two choices McIntyre. One, you kill me, and you keep the co-ordinates. But my sniper shoots a bullet right between your sister's eyes." laughed The Shogun while pointing two of his fingers to the centre of his forehead and imitating a gun.

"Two, you give me the co-ordinates and we let you and your sister go. So, McIntyre, what is it going to be?" asked The Shogun watching McIntyre closely.

McIntyre looked over to the helicopter. The Shogun will surely destroy us all if he gets the co-ordinates, he thought to himself. However, he couldn't risk the threat to his sister's life.

"Two, of course." said McIntyre quickly.

"Good decision Mr McIntyre. Now the co-ordinates please." said The Shogun holding out his hand.

McIntyre looked again at Emma in the helicopter, then reluctantly handed over the cylinder with the co-ordinates.

"I know you will come after us Mr McIntyre. If you do, I warn you there will be no mercy." shouted The Shogun.

The Shogun and his bodyguards then quickly disappeared from the rooftop restaurant.

McIntyre stood up and started to walk away.

"Hey asshole! You forgot your gun." shouted The Shogun's chief bodyguard.

McIntyre sized the man up. He was small for a bodyguard.

"And what do they call you? YoJimbo?" mocked McIntyre.

"My name is Hitoshi." the bodyguard replied.

"Whatever!" McIntyre grunted picking up his gun and he walked away.

McIntyre knew if he retaliated, they would kill Emma. What else could he do. He headed back to the elevator.

From the cockpit of the helicopter Emma watched her brother leaving and was confused as to what was going on. It wasn't what she was expecting him to do. What did he give The

Shogun? Emma wondered. She signalled with her hands to the pilot to turn around.

McIntyre made his way back to his suite and picked up his belongings and the laptop, then headed down to the lobby and checked out of the hotel. He was about to enter a taxi when he saw Emma directly in front of him.

"Damn it Emma! What do you want now?!" yelled McIntyre.

"The co-ordinates obviously." replied Emma.

McIntyre walked towards his sister. "You know, I'm a little bit tired of that question." he said to Emma dryly.

"You didn't give them to The Shogun, did you?" asked Emma not wanting to hear her brother's answer.

"Maybe." McIntyre said awkwardly. "I'll explain later."

"Oh my God! Fergus really!" she screamed at him.

"Listen. It's OK." said McIntyre trying to calm Emma down, and he ushered her away from the front entrance of the hotel.

"Fergus you just gave the biggest terrorist of the century the location to a load of bombs! How the hell can it be OK!" shrieked Emma at her brother.

"What I mean is I have a copy of the co-ordinates. They're on my laptop and I think we have the advantage." said McIntyre.

"What are you talking about?" asked Emma.

"I know the location of the bombs. They're in Edinburgh." explained McIntyre.

CHAPTER ELEVEN

EDINBURGH

A blanket of grey mist lingered over the city skyline and a faint drizzle of rain began to fall.

From his room window at the Balmoral Hotel McIntyre could barely make out Edinburgh Castle high on the rock. He did however have an excellent view over the glass roof of Waverley Station.

His thoughts then turned to his sister.

Before leaving Singapore, he had time to explain to her why he gave The Shogun the co-ordinates and why he had no choice but to just walk away. Together they came to an agreement to work together to stop The Shogun.

Finding the exact location of the hidden bombs was going to be tricky. He could do with someone on his side. Someone he could trust.

McIntyre continued to look down over Waverley. It was Britain's second largest railway station and its enormous roof which held thousands upon thousands of panes of glass covered a vast area of the city centre.

He quietly observed the coming and going of trains. There was a constant pulse of movement from commuters, rushing here there and everywhere.

As the light from the day drew to an end, flickering streetlights turned on one by one and brightened up the dull city skyline.

. . . .

Emma and an entourage of black SUVs arrived at the Balmoral Hotel. She got out of her car and leaned towards the window on the driver side.

"Wait here." instructed Emma to her driver. "I'll go alone. Yes, he's dangerous, but he is my brother. I know how to handle him."

At the front entrance of the hotel was a kilted concierge. He politely greeted Emma as she passed through an old-fashioned revolving doorway. She entered the grand lobby, walked past the reception, and stepped into the lift. Her head was spinning. What was her brother planning? How can we stop The Shogun? More importantly where exactly were the hidden bombs?

………..

McIntyre heard a knock on his hotel door. He picked up his gun and peered through the spy hole and slowly opened the door to greet his sister.

"Hello Sis." said McIntyre casually welcoming his sister. "Did you have a safe trip?"

Emma entered the room and McIntyre went back to his seat next to the window.

"Never mind my journey Fergus. Tell me where the bombs are." said Emma impatiently.

"I take it you and your team are willing to work with me this time?" asked McIntyre.

"Yes Fergus. Now, where are they!?" snapped Emma.

McIntyre lifted his hand and pointed downwards to the glass roof of the station.

"Fergus stop wasting time. It's the one thing we don't have." said Emma trying to implore with her brother.

McIntyre's eyes widened and he pointed again.

Emma approached the window and looked down.

"Oh. I see. So, what's the plan?" asked Emma.

McIntyre looked up at his sister and smiled.

"You brought some toys with you, didn't you?" he said grinning.

Emma sighed and rolled her eyes.

"Yes Fergus, but first I want to know where the bombs are, and what the plan is." Emma stipulated.

McIntyre stood up and started to walk round the room.

"Well," said McIntyre and he took a deep breath. "The thing is, we don't know the exact location. They've been hidden for some time and finding them is going to be difficult. You better get your team up here so we can brief everyone together. You do trust me Emma, don't you?" he asked.

Emma stared hard at her brother. She wondered whether he had any idea what he was doing or if he was just making it up as he went along. But he had been right before, and she had faith in him.

"Ok Fergus. I'll contact them." said Emma

Emma lifted her mobile phone to her ear. "Bring everything." she said. She then turned to face her brother. "My job is on the line Fergus. This better be good."

Several NCA officers then entered the hotel, each one carrying a large briefcase. They walked past the reception and made their way to the lift. Soon they came flooding into McIntyre's hotel suite and stood in silence waiting for their next instructions.

McIntyre cleared his voice "Ok. Here's the plan. The bombs are not in the station."

Emma stared at her brother aghast and opened her mouth to speak. McIntyre quickly lifted his hand to stop her from interrupting.

"The bombs are not in the station." continued McIntyre. "But they are hidden underground. There are several vaults and tunnels to lead us there and the only entrance to reach them is through the station Booking Hall. That's the building with the dome roof." explained McIntyre.

McIntyre then moved towards the window and pointed down to the glass roof of Waverley Station.

"I went down there today to get a better look and took the opportunity to take some pictures which I have here." said McIntyre.

McIntyre opened his laptop a pressed the keypad to display the images on the screen.

"The bombs were confiscated from the Japanese in 1945 and secretly hidden here in Edinburgh underground." explained McIntyre, he pressed the keypad on his laptop to reveal a picture of a door.

"However, the Japanese managed to track the bombs and concealed the coordinates inside a Katana sword, which was then lost through time, until now." said McIntyre.

"Yes! Yes! Fergus, we know all that. What we want to know is where are the bombs?" asked Emma impatiently.

McIntyre paused and looked down at the screen.

"This is the door we must take to reach the bombs. It looks like any kind of door, however if you look closer, you'll see it's not." explained McIntyre, and he used his thumb and forefinger to enlarge the picture on the screen.

"The door appears to have six locks." said McIntyre.

Emma interrupted him again. "So, we need to find six keys to open it. And where do we find the keys?" she asked.

"Well Emma, if I knew that, I wouldn't be asking for your help, would I." McIntyre replied sarcastically.

Emma bit her tongue and sat quietly hoping her brother had a plan.

"Can we not just blow it?" blurted out one of the officers.

Emma rolled her eyes at the officer "What?!! And blow up the entire city of Edinburgh along with half a million of its residents! There are bombs down there remember!" she said frustratedly and rolled her eyes.

McIntyre waited for Emma to calm down, then continued. "The Shogun could have easily done the same, but he hasn't. I suspect he will want to remove the bombs and use them for another purpose or to have a bigger impact."

McIntyre returned to the laptop and pointed at the screen. "If you look closely, you'll see each lock has an image above it. A crown, a crucifix, a water droplet, a saltire, an apple, and a gun." he explained.

Emma shook her head. 'How were they going to beat The Shogun now?' she thought.

"Come on Emma." encouraged McIntyre. "We can do this. Remember when we were kids, we used to solve puzzles all the time."

Emma gave her brother a half smile.

"Look closely at the crown lock. There isn't actually a keyhole, but it has text below it and the other ones don't." said McIntyre and he enlarged the picture again. "It's some sort of riddle or call it a quest if you like."

McIntyre went on to read the text out loud. "Follow the cattle down to the market and at the gate meet your King."

The room went quiet. Everyone's lips were quietly muttering the words McIntyre had just read out.

Emma paced around the room and joined in with the muttering. McIntyre watched her closely, he was confident she would solve the riddle quickly. His sister was clever at school particularly in Scottish history. Forgotten battles, folklore and fables were her area of expertise.

"George the Fourth Bridge!" Emma blurted out excitedly. "It goes over the Cowgate!"

"Of course," said McIntyre pleased his sister had solved the riddle. "I told you we had the advantage. The Shogun is not going to know Edinburgh like we do. Ok, great, we'll start at the Cowgate."

"Wait, how do we know where the other five keys are?" asked one of the NCA officers.

"I don't know." answered McIntyre. "I guess we'll get more clues as we progress." he said and shrugged his shoulders.

Another officer stood up and waved his hands in the air "Whoa! Whoa! You guess?" he asked mockingly. "Ok, I don't think you know what you're doing. We should…."

"Hey!!" yelled Emma interrupting "He knows a damn sight more than any of you! I trust him. So, I suggest you do the same too."

"Thank you, Emma." said McIntyre appreciating his sister's faith in him.

There was a moment silence. McIntyre sighed heavily and continued his briefing.

"To add into the mix of our problems, The Shogun and his associates will be wanting to get their hands on the keys too. They will be watching us closely." said McIntyre.

"Just to be clear The Shogun said he will show no mercy. And we can't afford any mistakes. So, I need you guys to stay here as back up. Emma and I will go to the Cowgate alone." instructed McIntyre.

"I don't think that's a good idea." said one of the officers.

"It's OK. We will both have tracking devices on so you can keep tabs. If we need you, we will contact you, so keep your coms on. Besides, we need you to clean up any mess in our wake." assured Emma.

McIntyre looked down to the table where his gun was resting, a small glint of light on the base of the hand grip of his gun caught his eye.

"What the hell!!" shouted McIntyre.

McIntyre picked his gun up to get a closer look. There was a small silver disc attached. He recalled the conversation he had with Hitoshi on the rooftop in Singapore. Hitoshi must have placed the disc, which was a microscopic microphone, on his gun before handing it back to him.

Everyone in the room stared at McIntyre.

"We need to move fast! This meeting has been tapped." explained McIntyre.

McIntyre removed the tiny microphone from the base of his gun and showed it to Emma. He then dropped the disc on the floor and crushed it with the heel of his shoe, destroying it.

"Ok! let's get moving!" urged Emma to the other officers.

There was a flurry of movement in the hotel room as the officers set up their equipment from the large briefcases they had brought into the hotel.

Emma approached her brother.

"I almost forgot. We have a company car for you." said Emma and she handed her brother a key. "Press this button and the car comes to your location. Please don't wreck it. It's quite expensive." she said cautioning her brother.

McIntyre took the car key and nodded his head appreciatively. He then turned his attention to the military briefcases. One by one he opened them. Looking at the contents McIntyre smiled, he felt like all his Christmases had come at once.

One of the officers moved alongside McIntyre then proceeded to inform him of the contents.

"AAC Honey Badger, Sub sonic mags, equipped with red laser and thermal sight. Over here we have black op flash grenades. Here we have a Glock 44, with a laser sight and …" The officer paused then opened a smaller briefcase. "Here are your mags for the Honey Badger and your handgun." the officer finally said handing over the equipment.

"Thank, you, very, much!" said McIntyre emphasising each word.

"Happy hunting Mr McIntyre." said the officer.

"Thank you. You certainly know your stuff." said McIntyre to the officer.

McIntyre looked up at the officer he was talking to. He looked familiar. The officer then winked at McIntyre and walked away.

McIntyre raised his eyebrows in surprise. It was Benson!

....

That evening The Shogun arrived at Edinburgh Waverley Station with his entourage.

Hitoshi and the other bodyguards stood silently waiting for their orders.

"Iriguchi o mitsukeru!" *(Find the entrance!)* The Shogun commanded.

Two of the Shogun's bodyguards set off in the direction of the Booking Hall. The Shogun then walked slowly back to the car park with his remaining entourage.

They approached three black Range Rovers. Hitoshi assisted The Shogun into one while the rest of the men separated into the other two cars.

"Iku!" *(Go!)* Hitoshi shouted at the driver of their car.

All three vehicles acerated and left the station at speed heading for the Cowgate.

The convoy of cars vibrated and skidded as they gripped the wet cobbles driving through a labyrinth of narrow streets.

In next to no time The Shogun and his men were at the Cowgate approaching the vaulted arch of the George IV bridge.

There was a dull thud which appeared to come from the last car in the convoy.

Puzzled by the sound Hitoshi looked behind, but he could not see anything unusual. Turning back round to face forward Hitoshi looked up at the bridge.

In the dark and through the drizzle of rain, he could make out the silhouette of a man on top of the bridge. An orange glow from a streetlight outlined the man's body. Hitoshi recognised him. It was McIntyre.

"Fuseru!!" *(Get Down!!)* yelled Hitoshi.

McIntyre took aim at the window screen of The Shogun's car and shot multiple rounds from his gun.

Then suddenly, there was a loud explosion. The last car in the convoy burst into flames and the other cars came to an abrupt stop.

The driver of The Shogun's car stepped out and took cover behind the open car door. He aimed his gun at McIntyre on the bridge above and fired several shots but failed to hit his target. McIntyre returned fire and instantly shot the driver.

The engine of The Shogun's Range Rover was still running. Hitoshi climbed into the front seat and accelerated the car towards the bridge. He pulled the handbrake hard and swerved the car under the arch of the bridge giving himself and The Shogun some protection.

Hitoshi got out the car and summoned another bodyguard to his car.

"Kare o eki ni tsureteiku!" *(Take him back to the station!)* Hitoshi ordered.

The bodyguard nodded, jumped in the driver's seat of The Shogun's car, and at speed drove the Range Rover away from the scene with The Shogun seated in the back.

……..

McIntyre looked down from the bridge and saw The Shogun's car drive off. He reached into his jacket pocket and pulled out the key Emma had given him and pressed a button on the fob.

In the distance he heard a whirring electrical noise. Almost immediately a car stopped in front of him.

The car was an electric Lotus Evija hyper car. McIntyre was impressed by the car his sister had lent him. He stood for a moment admiring the exterior. Its beautiful shape was intoxicating. The fluid forms of the car's dark blue body were configured with a pinstripe of white wrapping its way around the bottom of the car and it had aero alloy wheels as a finishing touch.

McIntyre had read about the car and was looking forward to driving it. The all-electric car was described as a stunning piece of automotive design and featured a dramatic Venturi tunnel through each rear quarter, giving it a truly breath-taking presence. It was able to race from 0-62 miles per hour in under three seconds and accelerate to a top speed of more than 200 miles per hour.

However, McIntyre didn't have time to look and admire the beauty of this machine. He had one objective and that was to stop The Shogun. He jumped into the driver's seat of the Lotus, grabbed hold of the rectangular steering wheel, and drove off through the dark streets of Edinburgh.

....

Emma emerged from the shadows of a doorway on the Cowgate. She held a device in her hand, it was a sticky-bomb launcher which she had used to deploy explosives on the last car of the convoy. She quickly discarded it down an open manhole on the street then made her way to the bridge.

Emma ran under the arch of the bridge and opened a door which led into a garage.

Hitoshi saw Emma and slid back the hammer on his gun. "Koko de mattete." *(Wait here.)* he said to the other bodyguards. He then followed Emma into the garage.

Emma walked slowly through the garage. The premises had not been used for some time, dust and debris covered discarded broken car parts and scrap cluttered every inch of the property.

'How am I going to find a key in here?' Emma thought to herself.

In front of her was a huge blank wall. There was something odd about its shape. She noticed a set of bricks protruding out slightly and approached the wall. Her hand was drawn to touch the bricks and she reached out and pressed on them. There was a knocking sound of several bolts unlocking. Startled by the sound, Emma quickly stepped backwards.

A hidden door in the wall opened revealing a bright white room beyond. She peered through the doorway. In the middle of the room was a glass cabinet.

Emma stepped forward cautiously into the room and slowly approached the cabinet. She felt like she was in some sort of surreal dream. 'Who built this place?' she thought to herself.

Looking into the cabinet Emma could see a key. She looked closer and saw that it had markings on it. There was a carving on the bow of the key, it was a cross, and engraved on the outside of the bow were the words 'The Grey Franciscan's Haunted Prison'.

Emma whispered the words out loud. "Franciscans Haunted Prison." Where on earth was this? She muttered the words over and over while pacing round the cabinet.

Searching in her mind Emma recalled some history about Franciscan monks. They were of a Christian religious order that adopted a lifestyle of poverty. The monks or friars were sometimes referred to as Minorites and would wear a grey tunic or religious habit. They would live a simple life often relying on the goodwill of the people to whom they preached.

But what had they to do with a Prison, and a haunted one at that?

Emma stopped suddenly and smiled, then said out loud, "Of course, Greyfriars! And The Covenanters Prison."

Emma looked back at the key and pressed her hand against the glass cabinet. She was pleased another riddle was solved, but how was she going to get the cabinet open.

A dark shadow appeared in the reflection of the cabinet and Emma quickly turned around.

"ARGH!!!" screamed Emma.

Hitoshi grabbed Emma's hair. He quickly dragged her out of the room and back into the garage.

Kicking and screaming Emma tried to release Hitoshi's grip, but he was too strong for her. Hitoshi pulled Emma through the doorway and hurled her across the oily garage floor.

Emma staggered to her feet, raised her arms, and managed to block Hitoshi's next move. Without hesitating she then kicked him abruptly between his legs.

Hitoshi stopped dead in his tracks then collapsed to the ground in agony. He lay on the garage floor squirming and shielding his groin with his hands.

Emma saw her chance to escape. She picked up a brick, ran back into the white room and smashed open the glass cabinet then grabbed the key.

Returning to the garage Emma scanned her surroundings. Her eyes then locked on several propane gas cylinders. She backed up to a safe distance and shot two bullets at the cylinders.

There was an almighty explosion as the garage burst into flames.

The force of the explosion propelled Emma backwards through the garage doors and out onto the street.

Lying on the ground Emma turned round to see the garage engulfed in flames. The bodyguards waiting outside for Hitoshi lay unconscious on the ground beside her. She reached into her jacket pocket and pulled out her hand. Then slowly opening her clenched fist she looked down at the key.

Emma tried to stand up but found herself stumbling and disorientated by the explosion. She did not have time to waste, she had to get to the graveyard.

On the floor of the garage Hitoshi lay motionless under rubble and ash. His hand then suddenly twitched. Slowly he managed to sit up. Gathering all his strength he scrambled through the wrecked garage.

Hitoshi then limped his way out onto the street. He lifted his mobile phone to his ear.

"Bochi ni iku, Greyfriars." *(Go to the graveyard, at Greyfriars.)* he instructed in a crackling voice.

Hitoshi slumped down on the pavement exhausted. He lifted his trembling hand towards his face and flinched in pain. Half of his face was scorched and bleeding.

"Fukushū o shimasu." *(I will get my revenge)* he muttered angrily under his breath.

CHAPTER TWELVE

THE COVENANTERS KEY
GREYFRIARS KIRK

The Shogun sat quietly in the back seat of his Range Rover on Waverley Bridge. He drummed his fingers rhythmically on his walking stick mimicking the sound of the rain.

The Shogun's driver sat in the front seat holding a mobile phone to his ear listening to someone talking. He then laid the phone down on the seat next to him and spoke to the Shogun.

"Watashitachi Greyfriars bochi ni ikanakereba narimasen." (*We must go to the graveyard at Greyfriar*s) said the driver.

"Sate, ikimashou! Nande matteru no?!" (Well, *let's go then. Why are you waiting?!)* ordered The Shogun.

A strange whirring noise started to build from the streets in front of them. The driver and The Shogun turned their heads in the direction of the noise.

Suddenly McIntyre's Lotus Evija car came into view. The rear end of the car skidded as it hurtled down the wet cobbles on Cockburn Street and approached Waverley Bridge. The front lights of the Evija looked menacing as they shone towards The Shogun's car.

Cursing through gritted teeth The Shogun shouted at his driver "GO! GO! GO!"

Immediately The Shogun's driver slammed the Range Rover into reverse. A high-pitched whine from the car engine reversing startled pedestrians trying to cross the road, sending them running back to the pavement for safety.

McIntyre pushed a button on his steering wheel. Two sentry guns deployed from the front of his car and started firing rapidly at The

Shogun's Range Rover. However, the gunshots simply sparked and flashed as they ricocheted off the car's bulletproof panelling.

The Shogun's driver skilfully drove the Range Rover in reverse up Waverley Bridge. On reaching the junction, he spun the car around onto Princes Street.

The street was busy and packed with taxis and buses. Tourists, meandering between the gardens and shops on Edinburgh's main street, quickly dispersed out of the way of the oncoming cars.

McIntyre pulled hard on his handbrake and drifted around the corner following the Shogun's car onto Princes Street.

McIntyre then pressed a button on the dashboard of the Evija. There was a flicker of light and a digital projector appeared on his windscreen. He pushed another button on his steering wheel which deployed a smaller gun from the front wing of his car. Using the projector on the windscreen McIntyre targeted the wheels of the Range Rover and pressed the button again on the steering wheel. The gun fired a spear-like bullet which hit the tyre of the Range Rover and shredded it into pieces like rubber spaghetti. Black rubber sprayed all over the road and hit the windscreen of McIntyre's car.

The Shogun's driver instantly lost control of the Range Rover and crashed onto a pavement narrowly missing a group of people waiting at a bus stop.

McIntyre stamped on his breaks and screeched his car to a halt. He opened the butterfly wing door of the Evija and grabbed his gun. Before abandoning his car, he pressed the key fob. The doors of the Evija closed then the autonomous car drove off by itself.

McIntyre ran towards The Shogun's Range Rover. He slid back the hammer on his gun intending to finish The Shogun off.

Onlookers, on seeing McIntyre's gun, quickly ran and fled the scene that was unfolding in the city centre.

McIntyre reached the Range Rover and aimed his gun inside. The Shogun and the driver were gone. 'How could they just disappear?' he puzzled.

McIntyre then heard shots and more screaming. He turned round to see people pouring out from a side entrance of the railway station. He immediately headed in that direction. He reached the entrance which was at the top of a staircase and looked down. People were panicking and running in all directions. He saw the two figures of The Shogun and the driver pushing their way through the crowd of people.

McIntyre lifted his phone and contacted Emma. "I've got a visual on The Shogun!" he shouted trying to be heard above the noise of people surrounding him.

"They're going for the next key Fergus! It's in the prison at Greyfriars!" said Emma shouting back.

"OK, I'll meet you there. But first I'm going after The Shogun." replied McIntyre.

Inside the station The Shogun stopped at the top of an escalator. He turned to face his driver then gave him some instructions.

"Watakushijishin chika ni iku" (*I shall go underground*) said The Shogun. "Anata ga mitsukenakereba naranai kagi!" (*You must go and get the key.*)

The driver acknowledged The Shogun with a simple nod, then kept watch as The Shogun slowly descended the escalator.

McIntyre pushed his way down through the mass of people at the top of the steps. He stopped when he lost sight of The Shogun and the driver.

138

Standing still, McIntyre searched with his eyes through the throng of people in front of him. His eyes then fixed on the driver.

Realising he had been spotted the driver moved quickly away from the escalator.

McIntyre pressed the button again on the key fob for the Evija. He returned the key to his pocket then chased after the driver through the station.

Both men pushed their way through the sea of people who all seemed to be heading in the opposite direction.

Darting and weaving their way through the gaps created between the bodies of people, the men eventually reached a balcony walkway.

McIntyre was gaining on the driver as they approached an exit. Suddenly out of nowhere the Evija car appeared in front of the exit.

The Shogun's driver reacted quickly. He somersaulted over the bonnet of the car then sprinted through an archway on the opposite side of the road and up Fleshmarket Close. McIntyre quickly followed behind.

The narrow passage was dimly lit and had a steep staircase which seemed to stretch on forever. McIntyre could make out the driver's figure in the shadows and fired his gun up the staircase but missed his target.

Sparks from the bullets fizzed into the dark and little bits of stone debris sprayed here and there off the walls. The driver stopped to turn round. He laughed at McIntyre, then carried on up the stairs.

McIntyre sighed heavily and stopped running, he looked like he had given up on the chase. Turning round he descended the steps and returned to the bottom of the staircase to the

Evija car. He calmly got into the driver's seat and drove off at high speed to Greyfriars.

………

Below the station The Shogun stood in front of a door. He was mesmerised by the dark passage that he was standing in. It had a ghostly, haunting feel to it. However, it felt strangely comfortable to him.

The Shogun noticed a sign on the door. Walking closer he saw a symbol on the sign.

"Batsu" said The Shogun looking at the symbol. His voice echoed down the passage. There was a short silence followed by a menacing laugh.

………

McIntyre arrived at Greyfriars. He could hear music and people chatting coming from the bar directly next door. Two men suddenly spilled out of the bar and onto the street singing happily.

McIntyre walked quietly past them. He turned up a dark, cobbled street and approached the main entrance into the graveyard. Standing still he peered through the black bars of the gate.

McIntyre looked back to check he wasn't being watched, he drew out his gun and attached a suppressor. Slowly he pushed the gate open and entered the graveyard.

His eyes searched through the dark cemetery which was lit only by the moon and faint lights from the street beyond the graveyard walls.

He could still hear the men singing in the street and the faint thump of music coming from the bar, which gradually faded as he walked on.

He eventually reached another gate with a small, printed sign displaying the words 'Covenanters Prison'.

McIntyre noticed the chain on the gate had been cut and at his feet a discarded padlock lay on the ground.

He looked through the gate and saw a silhouette of a man kneeling on the ground. It was The Shogun's driver searching for the key.

McIntyre opened the gate then stopped suddenly as the old, rusty hinges gave out a high pitch creak.

The driver turned his head sharply and looked towards the gate. His eyes narrowed as he peered through the dark. He quickly turned his attention back to finding the key again.

McIntyre stepped through the gate and took cover behind a tree. Slowly but surely, he moved closer to the driver using the open doorways of burial vaults as added cover. He stopped and watched the driver from a distance.

Feeling his way over the cold tombstones with his hands the driver continued to search for the key in the dark. A cloud of breath floated in front of the driver's face. Like a small vaporous ghost, the cloud then drifted upwards and vanished into the cold night air.

The driver placed his hand behind an ornate carved tombstone. He pulled out a small package wrapped in a dirty grey cloth, unravelled it, and revealed a key.

McIntyre wondered to himself how the driver knew where to look?

Hearing a noise behind him the driver quickly spun round. He raised his gun and stared into the dark. All he could see were the outlines of gravestone. Satisfied that no one was there, he started to walk back to the gate.

McIntyre swiftly ran up behind the driver and tackled him to the ground. The driver's lost his grip on the key and it soared through the air. When it came back down it rang like a bell as it hit the stony ground at McIntyre's feet.

McIntyre quickly picked the key up and stared at it. He examined the markings on its bow, he was able to make out an image of a droplet.

The driver kicked it out of McIntyre's hand. The men then fought furiously for minutes on end. Each one equally matching their skills in combat. Finally, they stopped fighting when they both tried to gain the advantage, and their limbs locked.

"Who the hell are you?!" shouted McIntyre aggressively and pushed the driver back. "How did you know where to find the key?" he asked.

"My name is Tsukushima!" the driver replied smiling and calmly took one step back. Suddenly he somersaulted backwards, with one leg extended he kicked McIntyre on his jaw and knocking him to the ground.

McIntyre dropped the key again which Tsukushima quickly grabbed then ran off towards the gate.

Emma finally arrived at the graveyard. She saw Tsukushima dart out of the Covenanters Prison. She raised her gun and fired, but it was dark, and her bullet strayed hitting a wall.

Tsukushima turned briefly and stared at Emma, then made his escape at the far end of the graveyard.

"Damn it!" she shouted angrily and ran as fast as she could towards the prison gates. She was relieved to see her brother still alive.

McIntyre sat up rubbing his chin "Argh. Did you get him?" he asked.

"No." said Emma regretfully. "Though it looks like he got you." she said looking at her brother.

"Tsukushima, The Shogun's driver found the key." said McIntyre

"How the hell did he know where to look?" asked Emma.

"I don't know." replied McIntyre. "I guess we shouldn't underestimate The Shogun and his men."

Emma then realised Hitoshi must have heard her in the garage when she found the first key. Hitoshi would have passed the information on.

"He must still be alive." said Emma realising what had happened.

"Who?" asked McIntyre.

"Hitoshi, he must have told the driver where to look." explained Emma feeling guilty about giving the location of the key away. "What now?" Emma asked her brother

"The Shogun's driver has the second key, but I managed to get a glimpse of it." said McIntyre still rubbing his chin. He stood up and slowly walked back to the gate.

"The key, it had a water droplet engraved on it and text around it. The words if I remember said 'From the North Lake no more, cometh the Shard.' said McIntyre trying to visualise the key in his head.

"What? There isn't a lake in Edinburgh" said Emma shaking her head. "You must have got it wrong." she insisted.

McIntyre stopped for a moment, then turned to his sister to speak. "There might not be lakes in Edinburgh, but there are lochs. In fact, there are several of them. St. Margaret's, Dunstapie, Lochend, Duddingston …"

"The Nor Loch!" shouted Emma interrupting her brother. "North Lake no more. It's the Nor Loch. They drained it years ago, it's now the gardens on Princes Street!" said Emma excitedly.

"Shhhhhhhh!!!" hissed McIntyre angrily. "We don't know who's listening."

Emma silently mouthed the word 'sorry'. She then whispered, "The Shard, what's that then?"

"If the Nor Loch is the gardens, then it's got to be the Scott Monument." McIntyre guessed.

The chase was on to find the next key. McIntyre and Emma picked up their pace and exited through the main graveyard gates.

CHAPTER THIRTEEN

THE NOR LOCH KEY, PRINCES ST GARDENS, EDINBURGH

Hitoshi finally approached Princes Street Gardens. Directly in front of him he saw the huge, black, jagged image of the Scott Monument. It's gothic shape and elevated position dominated over central Edinburgh.

On reading the inscription of the second key Tsukushima and Hitoshi had worked out together the location of the third key. Now all they had to do was find it before McIntyre did.

Hitoshi entered the ticket booth at the monument.

151

A young tour guide leaned forward. "Sorry, we're closed." he said politely. "Perhaps you can come back tomorrow. We open again at ….." he suddenly stopped talking when he saw Hitoshi's burnt and blistered face.

"Take me up." growled Hitoshi at the young tour guide.

"Erm, did ye no hear me man? We're closed!" said the young tour guide speaking in his thicker than usual Scottish accent to get his point across.

The young tour guide leaned a little further forward and stared at Hitoshi's face. "By the way, huv ye seen yer face mate?" he asked arrogantly and smirked.

Hitoshi lifted his gun and pointed it directly at the tour guide's forehead.

The young man's smirk disappeared quickly, and his mouth dropped open.

"Yes, I have seen my face, mate!' Hitoshi replied angrily through clenched teeth. "Shall we?" he said and flicked his wrist with the gun, waving it in the direction of the stairs.

....

Emma and McIntyre arrived back at the Balmoral Hotel.

"Go to my room, get more ammo and some backup." instructed McIntyre.

"Where are you going?" Emma asked.

"I'm going after the next key." replied McIntyre and he pointed at the huge black monument in front of them.

McIntyre made his way quickly along Princes Street towards the monument. It wasn't long before he reached the entrance to the gardens where the monument stood.

He entered the monument ticket booth. A sign on the desk said closed and there was no one there. Turning around he noticed the entrance door to the monument was partially open.

Carefully he pushed at the door and stepped inside. In front of him was a narrow spiral staircase leading up to other levels. He pressed his back against the stone wall, pointed his gun up the stairwell and slowly started to climb the steps.

McIntyre stopped abruptly. He could hear some commotion and then a muffled scream. He ran up the remaining stairs and exited out onto a small outdoor terrace. The noise was coming from behind a door which led to the monument Museum Room. Without hesitating McIntyre kicked the door open.

It was dark inside except for some dappled multicoloured light produced from the stained-glass windows encircling the room. The light illuminated a body lying motionless on the floor.

McIntyre put his gun down and quickly leaned over the body to check for a pulse. It was the young tour guide; he was knocked unconscious and badly beaten. Beside the young man was an upturned display cabinet and broken glass from the casement was scattered all over the museum floor

Out of the shadows Hitoshi suddenly appeared behind McIntyre.

Hitoshi grabbed McIntyre by the neck and dragged him back outside onto the terrace. McIntyre managed to free himself from

Hitoshi's grip, then the two men began a frenzied fight.

The terrace was lit with spotlights and the dark night sky backdropped the men's fighting figures. The scene resembled an elevated boxing ring in a heavyweight championship. Except no one was spectating. The traffic below continued to flow along the busy street and passers-by walked on unaware of the furious fight taking place above their heads.

The men's arms and legs sliced through the air in perpetual motion trying to block each other's next move.

The speed of the fight was intense. Each blow to their bodies came fast and hard. Each man reacted accurately deflecting their opponent's attack.

The smooth chain of combat movements looked seamless, appearing automatic, almost robotic.

The arms of both men then became intertwined and locked.

McIntyre drew his opponent closer to him then delivered a vicious head butt onto the bridge of Hitoshi's nose.

Hitoshi stumbled backwards and held his hands up to his face. Blood burst out of his nose and into his cupped hands. He looked back at McIntyre. Rage spread over his mutilated face.

Hitoshi lunged forward at McIntyre but lost his balance. His back hit a railing. Hitoshi's arms flaying erratically in the air for a moment then he flipped backwards over the barrier.

With his arms outstretched, Hitoshi managed to cling onto the hard, jagged stone surface of the monument.

McIntyre returned to the Museum Room and retrieved his gun. Calmly he approached the edge of the terrace and looked down over the railing. He aimed his gun down at Hitoshi and squeezed the trigger. There was a short, sharp click. He was out of ammunition.

Hitoshi smirked back up at McIntyre. His life for now was spared. Gripping onto the intricately carved stonework he started to climb back up.

McIntyre stood on the terrace watching Hitoshi swinging and swaying about while attempting to climb. He prepared himself for another onslaught of fighting.

While Hitoshi moved about McIntyre noticed the key drop out of Hitoshi's pocket. There was no need fight now, the key was all he required. He quickly moved back inside to the Museum Room and lifted the tour guide up onto his feet, then together they made their way back down the spiral stairs.

The young man was shaken and had blood and bruises all over his face.

"You'll be fine." said McIntyre and helped the tour guide back into the ticket booth.

McIntyre then left the tour guide and ran outside onto the grass below the monument. 'This wasn't going to be easy' he thought as he searched through the dark on the wet ground looking for the key. It was like looking for a needle in a haystack.

Just then, a light from passing traffic glinted on something metallic and revealed the keys position.

McIntyre picked up the key, then looked up to the terrace on the monument. Hitoshi had disappeared. Quickly he made his way back round to the ticket booth.

"He went that way!" shouted the young tour guide pointing along a path.

Staring down the long path towards the National Gallery McIntyre could see the figure of Hitoshi limping away in the distance.

Just then McIntyre's phone rang. It was Emma.

"I've got the key." said McIntyre answering out of breath.

"Great Fergus. Where to now?" Emma asked.

McIntyre held the key up and looked at it closely. Engraved on the outside of the bow were the words 'Look to the House on the Hill'. He turned the key over and the words continued. 'Through War, Peace & Change it stands still.' In the bow of the key was the image of a Flintlock Gun.

McIntyre's focus then looked beyond the key. In the distance he could make out the silhouette of Edinburgh Castle sitting high on the edge of the rocky cliff.

"Emma, it's the Castle. Go there!" instructed McIntyre. He immediately finished his conversation and began to make his way down the long path through Princes Street Gardens.

....

Hitoshi reached the end of the path next to the gallery. He hobbled his way over to a parked car, sitting in the driver's seat was Tsukushima.

"Kī o nakushita. Ī nda yo." *(I lost the key, but it does not matter.)* said Hitoshi getting into the car.

"Mita koto arimasu. Shiro made doraibu!" *(I saw it. Drive to the castle!)* Hitoshi ordered.

Tsukushima put the car into gear and sped off up the hill towards the castle.

CHAPTER FOURTEEN

THE FLINTLOCK KEY, EDINBURGH CASTLE

McIntyre ran down the path towards the National Gallery. Hitoshi was nowhere to be seen; it was as if he had vanished into thin air. McIntyre did not have time waste searching for Hitoshi, he needed to get to the castle and find the next key.

Running up the side of the gallery was a long flight of stone steps. McIntyre sprinted up the stairs leaping two or three treads at a time and quickly reached the top. He ran across the road, entered a dark alleyway, then continued up another steep flight of stairs.

Eventually he reached the top and exited out of the alleyway onto the Lawnmarket. He stopped for a moment to reassess his bearings and catch his breath.

Ahead of him was the imposing Tollbooth Kirk. Like many places of worship, the building was now used for another purpose. A crowd of young people gathered at its doorway queuing to get in to dance to the loud music pumping out from within.

Beyond the Kirk was the castle esplanade. McIntyre walked past the crowd and up the hill to the castle. The street darkened and narrowed the further he walked along. The buildings on either side felt like they were closing in on him. McIntyre narrowed his eyes. He heard a noise to his left and turned his head round sharply but couldn't see anything. Just an old door creaking open and shut with the wind.

The loud music from the Tollbooth Kirk was now just a muffled throb. From a nearby restaurant a low chatter of voices floated in the night air and the soft light of flickering candles danced through bullion glass windows.

McIntyre slowed his pace down. His senses heightened, he felt sure he was being watched.

There was a faint sound of footsteps. McIntyre stood still then everything went silent.

McIntyre reached into his jacket pocket for his gun, then remembered he was out of ammo.

Just then he felt a hand on his shoulder.

McIntyre quickly grabbed the hand and flipped the body of a man over his shoulder. The man landed on the cobbled road with a thud. McIntyre then knocked him out swiftly with one punch.

Another man suddenly appeared in front of McIntyre blocking his path to the castle. McIntyre sized him up. This man was smaller than the last but heavier built.

McIntyre took a deep breath. He was tired of fighting but mustered all his strength and ran straight at the man standing in his way. As he moved forward, he sidestepped, pressed his foot against a wall and propelled himself upwards, then swiftly hook kicked the man on his jaw.

The man stumbled and fell to one side, then lost his balance and tumbled down a stone staircase, eventually he came to an abrupt stop and hit his head hard on a step.

McIntyre watched emotionless from the top of the stairs. He waited to see if the man would get up. A pool of blood seeped slowly from the man's head across the stone step where he lay.

Suddenly there was a rumble over the cobbled road. McIntyre swung round quickly to see a V8 Range Rover driving straight at him. The car stopped in front of him, and a tinted window lowered. It was Emma.

"You're a bit late with the backup Emma." said McIntyre sarcastically and he glanced at the two officers in the back seat.

"Yes. Looks like you managed fine without us." replied Emma observing the lifeless men on the ground.

McIntyre got into the Range Rover then Emma drove up the esplanade to the castle entrance.

On their approach to the castle, they saw two guards lying dead on the ground. The huge, armoured door at the gatehouse was also open.

Anticipating that more trouble lay ahead; McIntyre, Emma and the two officers suited themselves up with the weapons Emma had brought with her from the hotel.

They made their way through the gatehouse door and up the hill to the castle Portcullis. This gate was also open and unguarded. Although the castle was closed for the evening there should have been several guards on duty.

'Where was everyone?' thought McIntyre.

They progressed cautiously up the cobbled hill and moved further into the castle grounds, covering each other's backs until they reached an open square at the heart of the castle.

A light was shining from one of the buildings.

"They're in the Great Hall" whispered Emma.

McIntyre turned to the two officers who accompanied them. "You two stay out here." he instructed in a low voice.

Emma and McIntyre approached the heavy oak door to the Great Hall. It was ajar. McIntyre slowly pushed the door open and stepped inside.

High above their heads, giant wooden beams suspended several ornate chandeliers which illuminated the hall. The upper half of the walls were painted a bright crimson red and the lower half clad with wooden panelling. An impressive display of military weapons and medieval armoury covered every inch of the walls.

Emma and McIntyre walked slowly around the hall. McIntyre looked down at the paved floor and saw small drops of blood. 'Someone has been here' he thought and suspected Hitoshi.

McIntyre remembered the image of a Flintlock gun on the key. He scanned the walls and saw a spherical display of pistols on a wooden panel. The display was so ornate that anyone would have mistaken it as a wood carving.

Twelve guns were exhibited in the circle. McIntyre looked closely at each gun. One of the guns he noticed was smeared in blood. He pulled at its wooden and brass stock handle.

There was a creaking noise which was followed by a mass of mechanical sounds. The noise reverberated through the walls then channelled its way to the large fireplace at the other side of the hall.

Emma and McIntyre looked at each other, then together they slowly approached the fireplace. Their eyes widened as the hearth opened slowly. But all they found was an empty space.

"What the hell?!" shouted Emma.

Just then they heard two loud gunshots. McIntyre and Emma sprinted outside to find one of the officers was dead and the other badly wounded. Emma knelt beside the wounded officer who mumbled and pointed in the direction of the gunfire. McIntyre looked up to see two recognisable figures disappear around the corner.

Without hesitation McIntyre followed them. Emma, concerned about her colleague, made the officer comfortable then quickly caught up with her brother at the castle esplanade.

The wide-open space of the esplanade made it easy for McIntyre to track his assailants down. They were running towards a car parked at the far end of the esplanade. McIntyre took aim and fired his gun.

The men stopped immediately as the bullet hit the ground in front of their feet. Then together they turned around to face McIntyre. It was Hitoshi and Tsukushima.

Although he was quite a distance away from the men, McIntyre could see clearly it was Hitoshi and Tsukushima. He winced at the sight of Hitoshi's burnt and bleeding face.

"Ooft!" said McIntyre turning round to see Emma by his side. "Look what we did to his face?" he quietly muttered.

"Yes, he doesn't look too happy." replied Emma

"What are you going to do McIntyres?! shouted Hitoshi.

"Look!" yelled Emma. "We've got two keys, and you have two keys! If you hand them over, we will free you from The Shogun!" she said trying to make a deal with the men and she moved slowly forward.

"You really think they're going to negotiate with us Emma?" asked McIntyre with a level of sarcasm.

Hitoshi and Tsukushima looked at each other puzzled by Emma's proposal, then laughed together. "You think we are slaves of The Shogun?!" asked Hitoshi. "Huh, you're so wrong!!" he said sniggering.

Hitoshi and Tsukushima turned their heads and looked further down the esplanade. They could hear sirens approaching.

"Did you call the Police?" McIntyre asked Emma angrily, briefly taking his eyes off his target.

"No, I did not!" answered Emma bluntly now getting annoyed at her brother's tone. "This is all a big mess anyway Fergus, maybe we should wait for the Police." she said.

"What?! You know we can't do that! We must stop The Shogun tonight, and that is just not going to happen if the local fuzz get involved!" snapped McIntyre.

"Well, we wouldn't be in this mess if you had returned to London instead of going to Singapore!" replied Emma sharply.

McIntyre stared hard at his sister. He could not believe what he was hearing.

"Remember Emma, I don't follow your orders. I went there to get a better understanding of The Shogun. He's not just controlling them you know." said McIntyre as he pointed at Hitoshi and Tsukushima, "There's more to all of this than just The Shogun's plans. Other criminal networks are involved. Sometimes Emma you need to look at the bigger picture." explained McIntyre.

Emma and McIntyre continued to argue.

Hitoshi and Tsukushima took this opportunity to make their escape. They first made a beeline for their car but then realised the approaching police were about to block them in. Quickly they changed direction and ran to the far side of the esplanade. They climbed up a memorial stone and jumped over a railing.

McIntyre caught sight of Hitoshi and Tsukushima making a run for it. He fired his gun at them but missed, stray bullets sparked and ricochet off the metal railing.

On the other side of the railing Hitoshi and Tsukushima tumbled down a steep grassy embankment. They reached a path which led them into Princes Street Gardens.

"Come On Emma! We need to follow them!" shouted McIntyre.

Emma hesitated. She could hear the sirens getting closer. Her instinct told her to wait for the Police, but her brother was being so demanding. She made a snap decision and decided to go with her brother's plan.

With sirens blaring and lights flashing a convoy of police vehicles came screeching into the castle esplanade just as McIntyre and Emma went over the railing and out of sight.

CHAPTER FIFTEEN

THE ADAM KEY, SCOTTISH NATIONAL GALLERY, EDINBURGH

Hitoshi and Tsukushima followed a steep zigzag path which lay in the shadow of the castle down to Princes Street Gardens.

Although Emma and McIntyre could have easily caught up with Hitoshi and Tsukushima, they kept their distance. They wanted the men to lead them to the next key. They observed Hitoshi and Tsukushima as they made their way through the gardens. The path eventually levelled out then rose upwards to a gate which exited out in front of the National Gallery.

"We're going round in circles." whispered Emma to her brother. McIntyre lifted his index finger to his lips to shush her.

Hitoshi and Tsukushima left the gardens, crossed over the road, and made their way to the gallery. McIntyre and Emma followed close behind, arriving at the main entrance of the building to find Hitoshi and Tsukushima had already gone inside.

Stopping for a moment at the gallery entrance, McIntyre checked his ammo and put a new mag into his gun. He nodded to Emma and together they entered the building through the huge, stone pillared doorway.

In the vestibule they saw a single guard lying unconscious on the cold marble floor. McIntyre gestured silently to Emma to stay close behind him, he then slowly opened the door to the main gallery room.

The gallery room was dimly lit, except for two white marble statues illuminated with spotlights which helped guide their way.

McIntyre and Emma walked slowly through the gallery. Large portraits hanging on the bright red walls looked down on them.

Emma looked up at a painting of a woman dressed in pink satin. She then looked at another portrait, then another.

'This place is eery' thought Emma to herself. She felt uneasy and was convinced their eyes were following her around the room.

McIntyre and Emma eventually came to a hallway at the far end of the gallery. There was a set of stairs leading downwards. McIntyre looked at Emma and pointed down. He pressed his back against the wall and slowly descended the stairs. Each step they took was silent and smooth.

At the bottom of the stairs was another gallery room, much smaller than the one above. Emma and McIntyre made their way to an opening. They then found themselves walking through a labyrinth of exhibition rooms. Their path twisted and turned. Not knowing what lay ahead or around the next corner they moved cautiously forward.

"Fergus." whispered Emma.

"What?" McIntyre quietly answered.

"What exactly are we trying to find?" asked Emma

"I'm not sure, but they came here looking for something. Let's just try and keep quiet." replied McIntyre.

Suddenly there was a loud thump. Emma jumped and held her breath.

McIntyre slowly entered the next room. He saw a painting lop-sided on the wall.

Emma then followed her brother and looked closer at the painting.

"It's called 'The Expulsion of Adam & Eve from The Garden of Eden'." whispered Emma reading the title plaque. She looked behind the painting but there was nothing there, just a blank wall.

McIntyre searched the rest of the room.

There was a loud gunshot and bullet hole appeared in the painting Emma was looking at.

McIntyre spun round to see Hitoshi with Emma in a headlock and his gun pointing at her head.

"Drop the gun!!!" snarled Hitoshi at McIntyre.

But McIntyre ignored him. Instead, he levelled his gun up to Hitoshi's head and walked calmly forward.

"DROP IT!!!!" Hitoshi shouted.

McIntyre continued to move forward. Hitoshi then pulled the trigger.

There was a sharp click from his gun. He had no bullets left. Hitoshi looked stunned.

"Déjà vu." said McIntyre remembering his own gun failing at the Scott Monument.

Hitoshi stood still in a state of shock.

Emma suddenly elbowed Hitoshi in the ribs, spun him round then pinned him by his neck against the wall. McIntyre impressed by his sister's self-defence moves lowered his gun and walked casually over to Hitoshi.

"We've got some unanswered questions." grunted Emma in Hitoshi's face. "And how the hell did you know there were no bullets in that gun!" snapped Emma angrily at her brother.

"Instinct." replied McIntyre calmly.

"You've got some moves for a little lady." said Hitoshi laughing at Emma.

Emma pressed harder on Hitoshi's neck.

"OK, OK!" gurgled Hitoshi.

McIntyre raised his hand to gesture to Emma that she could relax her grip. He then turned to face Hitoshi and asked, "So, what does The Shogun plan to do with the bombs, if he gets them?"

"The Shogun will get the bombs. He never fails." said Hitoshi coughing and clearing his throat. "He has good reason to get them and will stop at nothing until he has them. When the World War Two ended and Japan surrendered, The Shogun was not going to help anyone on the American side and was disgusted that anyone Japanese should do so. The Shogun, you see, was from Hiroshima, and so was his family. The death of his entire family enraged him and has haunted him whole life. His plan McIntyre is simple. He wants revenge." explained Hitoshi smiling.

"The Shogun has known for many years the bombs were hidden in Edinburgh, but he didn't know where exactly. He has studied the city, its history, its stories, and its people." continued Hitoshi and he began to snigger.

"The Shogun just needed someone to locate the bombs and help him find the keys." Hitoshi said looking straight at McIntyre.

"Yes. You McIntyre. You led The Shogun straight to the bombs. And now he will have his revenge." said Hitoshi now laughing hysterically.

McIntyre pushed Emma to the side and pressed Hitoshi harder into the wall, his knuckles turned white with the pressure.

Hitoshi, although struggling to speak managed to get a few words out. "Wait. Let me explain." he said coughing. McIntyre released his grip on Hitoshi and took a step back.

Hitoshi composed himself and continued to talk. "As you know the Americans have their nuclear base on the west of Scotland with consent from your government. Of course, when I say government, I mean Westminster. That was in the sixties and things have changed since then. Now your so called 'Quango' government here in Scotland is not happy about having the base in their waters and is committed to withdrawal of all nuclear weapons from Scotland."

Hitoshi stopped talking then started to smile. His smile was menacing and spread slowly across his face. McIntyre was getting irate, and he gave Hitoshi a hard kick.

"You have not told us anything we don't already know. Now talk!!" shouted McIntyre and he held his gun up level to Hitoshi's groin.

"OK, OK!" shouted Hitoshi alarmed at the location of McIntyre's gun. He took a deep breath and continued talking. "In negotiations with your government about the nuclear arms base in Scotland, the Americans divulged information they had uncovered about the Japanese bombs and their location. Up until recently, the location of the bombs was only known by a small number of high-ranking military personnel and were secretly hidden here in Edinburgh without the consent or knowledge of your people. Officials were supposed to gather in Brazil with Scotland's First Minister and other heads of state to discuss how to safely remove the bombs and hide them again. But I guess, someone tried to stop them." said Hitoshi, who could not help himself from grinning then he began to laugh again.

"So that's what that meeting was about in Rio." said McIntyre. He lowered his gun and tried to absorb what Hitoshi was telling him. "You hired Adebayo!" shouted McIntyre at Hitoshi.

"Yes McIntyre. We hire lots of people. Like our friend Alverez in Venice. You are also right about other criminal groups being involved. You never know who might be working for us or who might be listening. You found my microphone, yes?" asked Hitoshi.

"So, the location of the bombs McIntyre that must worry you. It seems your American friends have betrayed you McIntyre. Your allies, are your enemies!!" said Hitoshi continuing to laugh.

"What's that saying people use again? Oh yes 'An eye for an eye' …. You blow up our home! We blow up yours!" goaded Hitoshi.

Emma saw her brother's eyes fill with rage as Hitoshi persisted to laugh. McIntyre explode in a fit of anger and knocked Hitoshi out with one blow. Hitoshi's body immediately went limp and collapsed in a heap on the floor

Emma watched her brother as he paced round the room trying to calm down. She had seen him like this before. He was unpredictable when he was this angry. She worried he might do something stupid.

Emma went back to look at the painting. "It doesn't make any sense." she said trying to engage her brother.

McIntyre moved towards Emma's side and together they stood looking at the canvas. The bullet hole had damaged a small part of the top right corner, but other than that the painting was still intact.

"Maybe there's a clue in the picture." suggested Emma and she studied the images of Adam and Eve closely.

Emma was glad her brother had joined her, if she could keep him focused on the painting just for a little while it might calm him down.

Emma then turned around to discover Hitoshi had disappeared.

"Damn it!" shouted Emma. "He's gone!"

"And he's got the next key." said McIntyre infuriated.

"You mean this key." said Emma smiling, waving the key in front of McIntyre's face. She had almost forgotten about it while trying to distract her brother.

"How did you…? When …?" asked McIntyre baffled as to how his sister had the key.

"I might have done a little rummaging in Hitoshi's pockets when we were questioning him." replied Emma.

McIntyre shook his head, smiled at his sister, and gave out a short sigh of relief. "So, this is the key they found at the castle. Well let's have a look at it then," said McIntyre impatiently.

This time on the bow of the key there was an image of an apple. McIntyre read out the words engraved on the outside of the bow. "The origin of first man & woman is in God's Garden."

McIntyre flipped the key over and continued to read the text on the other side. "Immortalised in bronze her beloved victorious shall be."

Emma screwed up her face trying to think, then looked back at the painting.

"On the key it said, find the origin. What does that mean?" asked McIntyre

"The origin of the name Edinburgh is Eidyn. Perhaps the 'origin' is about the garden of Eden." Emma said surmising.

"This might be another clue," said McIntyre pointing at the small brass title plaque fixed to the frame.

Emma moved to McIntyre's side to get a closer look of the engraved plaque.

"The Expulsion of Adam & Eve from The Garden of Eden," said Emma reading the title again, then she continued. "Look, it says here the painting was commissioned for Catherine Sinclair, 6 Charlotte Square, Edinburgh. I'm pretty sure that's Bute House, which is now the official residence of the First Minister of Scotland," explained Emma.

"And ..." Emma said slowly drawing out her words while trying to piece the clues together. "The town houses on Charlotte square, including Bute House, were designed by the architect Robert Adam."

"There is also a garden in the centre of Charlotte square. Maybe it's got nothing to do with the painting or the house," said McIntyre.

"Would that garden be the garden of Eden?" Emma asked her brother.

McIntyre shrugged his shoulders. "I don't know. All I know is that we need to go to Charlotte Square now." replied McIntyre.

"But, 'Immortalised in Bronze'," said Emma "surely that's a sculpture, and there are plenty of them here in the gallery."

"Yes, and there are plenty of them outside too. Look, Hitoshi and Tsukushima have left the gallery. My guess is they are on their way to Charlotte Square. Which is exactly where we should be going. Now let's go!" shouted McIntyre.

Emma and McIntyre now had three keys. But they had to find Hitoshi and Tsukushima, get hold of the key they had and somehow stop them getting the next key

They quickly made their way outside and left the gallery.

CHAPTER SIXTEEN

THE SALTIRE KEY

Soon Emma and McIntyre were heading down George Street to Charlotte Square. They were very aware that Tsukushima or Hitoshi would be watching them closely and try to follow or attack them.

McIntyre spotted Tsukushima running out of a side street in front of them, he was also heading for Charlotte Square.

McIntyre open fire and shot Tsukushima in the leg. Tsukushima fell to the ground and cried out in pain. However, the shot did not stop him, and he quickly got up and proceeded to Charlotte square.

On reaching the square Tsukushima discovered the gate to the garden was locked. He quickly climbed over the railings and fell onto the grassy turf.

"He's heading for the statue!" shouted Emma.

McIntyre caught up with Tsukushima and followed him over the railings. He took aim and shot Tsukushima again, this time in the other leg.

Tsukushima collapsed on the ground.

McIntyre casually walked up to Tsukushima, stood over him and pointed his gun directly down at Tsukushima's head. Showing no emotion, or hesitancy he squeezed the trigger on his gun.

Tsukushima looked up at McIntyre then passed out.

Emma eventually caught up with them and pushed McIntyre to the side. "You didn't need to kill him Fergus!" she screamed disappointedly at her brother.

"I didn't kill him. He just passed out," replied McIntyre bluntly. He then walked over to the bronze memorial statue in the middle of the garden.

Emma knelt over Tsukushima's body. She saw his eye lids flicker and the rise and fall of his chest indicated to her he was still alive.

"It's just as well, there's quite a body count building up. Remember Fergus, I will need to explain all this later to the NCA," said Emma cautioning her brother.

Emma then searched Tsukushima's pockets and retrieved the 'Nor Loch' key. "This is the one from Greyfriars," said Emma. "We can open the door now."

"Not quite," said McIntyre. "Remember, we need five keys to open the door." He recalled the words again from the 'Adam' key. "Immortalised in bronze her beloved victorious shall be."

Emma joined her brother. She flopped down on a bench situated under the statue and looked up at the bronze figure of Prince Albert on horseback, now patinated a bright turquoise green from enduring the Scottish weather.

Emma smiled, then out of breath from running softly muttered, "Prince Albert. Queen Victoria's beloved."

McIntyre stepped over a small metal railing that surrounded the statue and climbed up on to the granite base of the memorial. He removed a torch from his pocket and studied the relief sculpture panels around the base.

"I can't see anything. This could be another red herring," said McIntyre frustratedly.

Rubbing his hand slowly over one of the smaller bronze panels, McIntyre gently pressed on the sculpture. There was a faint audible click and the panel opened to reveal a concealed chamber behind it.

McIntyre reached into the chamber. Inside was the last key.

"What does it say Fergus?" asked Emma eagerly

McIntyre shone his torch on the key. In the bow of the key was an image of a diagonal cross. He then read out words around the bow. "The painted King a Crux Decussata shall reveal." Turning the key over he continued reading, "Arms of Nihon unseen in clandestine Eden."

"OK. I understand the last part. Arms of Nihon, that's the Japanese bombs hidden underground in Edinburgh. But what's a Crux Decussata?" McIntyre asked Emma and sat down on the bench beside her.

Emma pointed to the bow of the key.

"The diagonal cross, that's a Crux Decussata. … It's also known … as a saltire … or Saint Andrew's cross." explained Emma still breathless from running and trying to speak.

"And the painted King?" asked McIntyre.

"Not sure." answered Emma. She took the key and torch from her brother's hand to have a closer look.

"The painted King. The painted King …" she muttered repeating the words over trying to think what it might mean.

"Fergus," whispered Emma, and she pointed to the far end of the gardens.

McIntyre looked over his shoulder and saw a number of dark silhouettes of individuals approaching.

McIntyre sighed. "More of The Shoguns friends, I presume," he said.

Putting the 'Saltire' key in his pocket McIntyre quickly pulled Emma up to her feet.

"Come on. We need to move again." McIntyre urged his sister.

McIntyre and Emma were prime targets for The Shogun's men now they had all the keys.

Running out of Charlotte Square, Emma and McIntyre made their way back to Princes Street gardens.

They heard gunshots from behind them as they crossed the busy road and into the gardens. Heading left through a gate they then descended some stairs and took a path which led to an ornate illuminated fountain.

McIntyre quickly turned around, took aim, and returned fire at the men following them.

"We're sitting ducks here." said McIntyre.

"Run Emma! Head for the bandstand, I will cover you!" shouted McIntyre to his sister and pointed to the building in the distance.

Emma did not hesitate and did as her brother asked.

McIntyre shot at the men approaching, but The Shogun's men continued to move forward.

'Where were they coming from?' thought McIntyre, they seemed to be multiplying.

McIntyre took cover behind some trees. He watched Emma head towards the bandstand.

One of The Shogun's men caught sight of Emma running along the path. She was an easy target for him. He stood still, aimed his gun then squeezed his trigger.

McIntyre saw the gunman taking aim and immediately fired a shot at him. The bullet hit the gunman's hand, causing his gun to fly out of his grip. Nevertheless, the gun had triggered.

For a moment everything seemed to go in slow-motion for McIntyre. He turned round to see his sister running along the long path.

McIntyre yelled out to her, "Run Emma! Run!"

The bullet meant for Emma missed her by a hairsbreadth as it whizzed past her shoulder and hit the bandstand wall in front of her.

Emma stopped abruptly and looked behind. Quickly drawing breath Emma continued as fast as she could to the bandstand and took shelter behind the stage wall.

McIntyre emerged from behind the trees. He attacked the gunman and wrestled him to the ground, then without hesitation McIntyre fired two close range shots into his chest.

McIntyre's focus began to unravel while thinking about how he could protect his sister. Angry and frustrated he fired his gun randomly into the dark.

It wasn't like him to lose his cool, his sister's safety had triggered some emotion in him. McIntyre felt shaky and a bit sick. He didn't like this feeling and he tried to regain his focus. He reloading his gun then ran down the path towards the bandstand to join his sister.

"Fergus, I'm alright!" Emma called to him.

McIntyre climbed up on to the stage and joined his sister behind the stage wall.

"We need to shake them off." said McIntyre relieved to see his sister. He tried hard not to show his emotions when he saw her face.

There was an uneasy silence in the gardens. Then all hell let loose.

Sparks from gunfire appeared through the gardens like fireworks in the dark. However, this was no time for celebrations.

Emma and McIntyre heard sirens and saw flashing lights from the police on the main road above the gardens. There was a loud ear-piercing squeal, then a police officer spoke through a handheld megaphone demanding those responsible for the gunfire to stop and give themselves up.

There was a still silence again.

Emma looked at McIntyre knowing full well what was about to happen. The Shogun's men turned their attention to the police and opened fire on them.

McIntyre signalled to Emma to follow him.

They made their way to the back of the stage and exited the bandstand through a door at the rear of the building.

Emma followed her brother along a path behind the bandstand. They then came to a gate which was locked and climbed over it.

Emma stood beside her brother on a small bridge over the railway line.

"Where are we? And where are we going?" asked Emma.

"We now have all the keys, and the Shogun's men are going to stop at nothing to get them. We need to get to Waverley Station undetected, so this is our best route. We're going to have to go through there." McIntyre explained and pointed down the railway track to a tunnel.

Emma's jaw dropped open, and she gasped. McIntyre swung himself over the side of the bridge and down a metal ladder onto the track.

Emma nervously followed her brother. When she reached the bottom McIntyre suddenly pushed her to the side and onto the gravel track. He fired his gun upwards.

A man's body came crashing down and landed with an almighty thud on the ground in front of them. It was one of The Shogun's men.

"We need to keep moving!" shouted McIntyre trying to be heard above the noise of gunfire. He walked off towards the tunnel.

Emma stared at the body lying on the ground. Her brother's coldness towards the dead man bothered her. His lack of emotion showed her just how much he had changed and how impassive he had become.

Picking herself up she ran as best as she could along the gravel path behind McIntyre. They reached the entrance of the tunnel and stopped.

The darkness of the night intensified the gloominess of the tunnel. McIntyre took out his torch and shone it down the track. The beam of light wasn't much but at least he could see a few feet in front of him.

Emma remembered there was a torch on her smartphone. She switched it on and held it up, blinding her brother with the bright light in the process. McIntyre screwed up his eyes and shielded them with his hand. Emma realised her mistake and sheepishly pointed her phone to the ground in front of her.

McIntyre looked behind Emma to check no one was following them, then entered the tunnel.

Dangerous as this was, McIntyre believed going through the tunnel was the best way to get to the station without being seen.

As they ventured further in, the noise from the gunfire in the gardens faded. The walls of the tunnel were wet, and a strong smell of damp and decay lingered in the air. Emma could see some light at the end of the tunnel which was reassuring but it was still quite a distance away.

All of a sudden there was a deafening blast from a horn on a passing train in the adjacent tunnel. Emma and McIntyre both stumbled on the uneven ground and covered their ears quickly. The blast of the horn resounded through the tunnel and continued to echo in their ears for some time.

Emma and McIntyre steadied themselves and continued along the track through the dark. Eventually they emerged out of the tunnel. There was still a bit of track to walk before they reached the station. After a while they came to a ramp at the end of a platform.

McIntyre stepped up on to the platform, dusted his trousers and jacket sleeves with his hands and stamped his feet to get rid of the dirt. Emma followed close behind repeating her brother's movements.

They walked at pace along the platform. McIntyre then pointed to a gateway on a wall.

"That's where we are going." he said to Emma nodding his head to the left.

Emma looked at the small opening in the wall. The entrance was closed with a barred iron gate.

"Where does it go?" asked Emma.

"To the Scotland Street Tunnel." replied McIntyre.

"It's part of an abandoned railway line. It goes deep underground and was used in the second world war as an air raid shelter. You could say it's the perfect place to hide. This entrance has been blocked off for some time now, so we'll have to find another way in." explained McIntyre.

"I've never heard of it. How do you know so much about it?" asked Emma.

"Let's just say I know a man who knows a lot about history and secret tunnels." said McIntyre referring to Woods his new Quartermaster.

"Interesting. Maybe you should introduce me to him sometime." said Emma intrigued.

"Come on." said McIntyre pulling at his sister's arm, and together they made their way into the centre of the busy railway station.

CHAPTER SEVENTEEN

SCOTLAND STREET TUNNEL

McIntyre and Emma arrived at the Booking Hall in the centre of Waverley Station. Inside the huge stone structure was a waiting area bordered with shops, kiosks, and a ticket office. Suspended high above their heads was the glass domed ceiling they had seen earlier from McIntyre's hotel room.

Emma walked behind her brother with her eyes focused upwards, fascinated by the impressive Victorian glass ceiling and its intricate details.

Commuters sat quietly in neat rows waiting for their journeys to start. Most of them had their heads bowed low preoccupied with their mobile phones, oblivious of the goings on in the outside world.

A woman's voice made an announcement over the station tannoy and few hanging heads glanced up to read the flashing text on the digital information board. Then gathering their belongings quickly several commuters stood up and hurriedly made their way to the exit.

McIntyre and Emma continued to walk swiftly through the waiting room, dodging the crowd of commuters who had suddenly sprung to their feet. They passed the ticket office, through an archway then stopped at a door marked 'Station Staff Only'.

McIntyre, looked around, then slowly opened the door.

On the floor in front of them were the lifeless bodies of several station staff. McIntyre noticed one of The Shogun's bodyguards also lay dead on the floor.

"Over here." said McIntyre standing in front of a metal doorway.

Emma moved to his side, stepping carefully over the bodies that lay scattered on the floor.

McIntyre opened the metal door and peered in. It was pitch black inside and he could not see a thing. Searching with his eyes he made out the top of a metal staircase.

Emma looked over her brother's shoulder.

"Ladies first." said McIntyre politely and he gestured to Emma to step through the dark doorway.

"Don't you dare!" replied Emma sharply.

McIntyre smirked. He picked up a large torch which was resting on a cabinet in the staff room.

"Here, you take this." McIntyre said, handing Emma the torch. He then went through the doorway first and down the staircase.

McIntyres footsteps clanged off the metal treads on the staircase and echoed on into the dark abyss. Emma followed nervously behind using the torch to light their way.

Slowly they descended further into the darkness, twisting and turning, round and round. The stairs seemed to never end. Suddenly Emma lost her balance and slid down multiple steps.

"Aaaagh!" screamed Emma. "This is a nightmare! Fergus surely there is an easier way?" she pleaded with her brother.

"No, sorry Emma, this is the only way." said McIntyre and held out his hand to help Emma up.

"Are you alright?" McIntyre asked.

Emma nodded. "Yes, I'm fine, but I have lost my gun. This isn't going well. I really think we should turn back Fergus and get help." she implored.

"We don't have time for that." answered McIntyre, he turned round and continued down the rest of the stairs.

Eventually they reached the bottom step. Before them, in the dark, lay a labyrinth of corridors and passages.

"Where are we?" whispered Emma.

McIntyre leaned towards his sister and quietly explained, "This is a passageway that leads to the tunnel I told you about earlier."

"The Scotland Street tunnel?" Emma asked.

"Yes. Now, you go in front, and I'll cover your back." said McIntyre. He pointed in the direction of where he wanted to go then stood behind his sister.

Emma swapped places with her brother and walked on slowly through the tunnel.

They walked down a central passage, from which several vaulted chambers opened on either side. Emma shone the light from the torch into each one as she passed, fearful that someone or something was going to jump out and attack her.

Unnerving loud rumbles and vibrations from trains moving in and out the station above made Emma all the more anxious. She had heard many sinister stories about what lay beneath the city of Edinburgh and it's grim and ghostly past. Tourists visiting Edinburgh would take part in group excursions underground where they would learn from a guide, about tortured souls, murders, and even supernatural beings.

Emma was not one for fearing the dark or believing in ghosts. However, here in the dark her head filled with disturbing images. Her eyes began to played tricks on her, throwing shadowy figures in front of her path. Her heart started to beat fast, and her breathing became rapid and erratic.

McIntyre put his hand on Emma's shoulder which made her jump.

"Are you sure you're alright?" McIntyre asked again.

Emma bent down, lowered her head, and waited till she caught her breath before replying.

"I don't like this Fergus. No one can reach us here. We are so far underground. I can't get a signal on my phone and it's so …spooky!" Emma said, finally admitting she was scared.

McIntyre crouched down to face Emma. He could see the panic building up in her eyes. He reached out and held her trembling hand.

"Remember Emma, when we were kids, I was scared of the dark and you would comfort me. You'd ask me what I was afraid of. I would tell you that I thought there was someone in the wardrobe, then you'd make me go and check. I hated doing it, but of course, there was no one there. You helped be face my fears. Be brave and don't spend time worrying about the unknown, that's what you taught me." McIntyre said trying to calm his sister.

McIntyre's mind flashed back to another childhood memory when he lived in the Scottish Borders. He would dare himself to walk into the dark 'Half Mile' tunnel, an old disused railway tunnel situated close to the town of Peebles. The murky wet walls and all-consuming darkness were not what most would consider an enjoyable experience. This was where he would test his nerve and what was to be the beginning of his training.

McIntyre knew his training was far different from his sister's and could understand how frightened she was. His attention turned back to Emma's breathing.

"Breathe in through your nose then out through your mouth, that should slow down your heart rate and breathing." McIntyre said reassuring his sister.

Still holding Emma's hand McIntyre stood up, then in one swift movement pulled Emma up onto her feet.

Emma breathed in through her nose then pursing her lips and breathed out slowly.

"Good, keep doing that. Not far now." said McIntyre. He held up the torch and carried on walking down the passage.

Emma joined her brother, although this time she walked beside him.

McIntyre knew Emma enjoyed conundrums. To take his sister's mind off her surroundings he started a conversation about the last key they had found.

"The painted King a Crux Decussata shall reveal." said McIntyre remembering the text on the key. "We haven't yet worked out the part about the King. What do think it means?"

he asked knowing his sister also loved her history.

Emma held onto her brother's arm for comfort.

"A crux decussata is a diagonal cross. It is used as a symbol or ensign in many countries and can mean different things. It can also symbolise a hazard which is believed to be a simpler version of the skull and crossbones. In Scotland the cross or saltire represents Saint Andrew, who is supposed to have been crucified on a diagonal cross." explained Emma.

Emma was feeling calmer and more focused. Talking about the cross had helped to distract her from the situation they were in. She continued her explanation to McIntyre. "Legend has it that Saint Andrew appeared in a dream or vision to a Pict king before he was about to go into battle. In the dream Saint Andrew told the king to look to the sky for a cross which would be a sign they would win. When the battle was in full swing a strange cloud formed in the sky like a cross giving the king's men confidence to carry on and they won. In gratitude the Picts then adopted Saint Andrew as their patron saint and the saltire cross became Scotland's national emblem."

"So why does it say, 'The painted King'?" asked McIntyre, he wanted to distract Emma as much as possible, and keeping her talking seemed to be working.

"Ah." said Emma giving a little laugh. "It is thought the name Pict comes from the Latin name Picti, meaning pictured or painted people. In the 3rd century ad, invading Romans gave the name to a tribe of people who once lived in the north east of Scotland. Their name may refer to their custom of body painting or tattooing. No one really knows for sure as their culture blends into myth and legend."

"It's interesting you mentioned earlier Saint Andrew." said McIntyre.

"Oh. Why?" asked Emma curiously.

"Well, the Scotland Street Tunnel goes directly under Saint Andrew Square." explained McIntyre. Emma and McIntyre stopped walking and looked at each other.

Suddenly there was a flash of light.

"What was that?" said Emma turning round quickly.

"I didn't see anything" replied McIntyre. "Your eyes must be playing tricks on you again."

"Ah! We're here." said McIntyre holding the torch up to expose a red metal doorway.

On the door was a sign with a diagonal cross and some faded words in large bold print.

"Bleeding Red Gate." said Emma reading the words. "What does that mean?" she asked.

"It's a code name. The Americans named it that. Behind this door are the bombs." explained McIntyre.

Emma and McIntyre paused for a moment. They looked at the door and the elaborate locking system. Each lock depicted an image above it and lay side by side in a horizontal line, starting with the crown imitation lock on the far left.

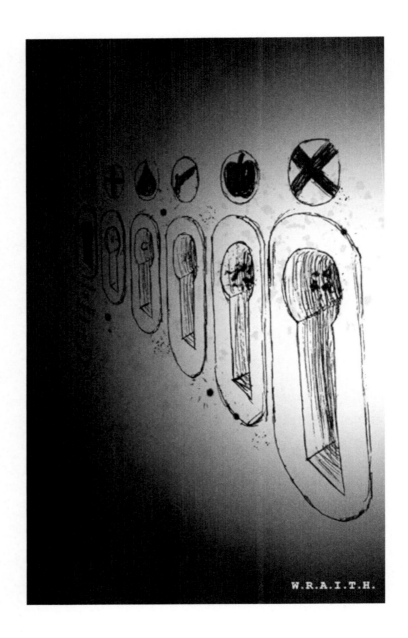

McIntyre searched in his pocket then held out two of the keys. "Do you have the other keys?" asked McIntyre.

"Yes. Here they are." said Emma collecting the three remaining keys from her pocket.

"Why don't we just leave the door locked?" asked Emma. "The bombs are still hidden, aren't they?"

"That would be easier. But I'm afraid we can't. Their location is now compromised." answered McIntyre and he held out his hand.

Emma passed the keys over and shone the torch on the door while McIntyre matched the keys one by one to the locks.

"Ready?" asked McIntyre.

Emma nodded. "Ready." she replied.

The locks were stiff and rusty and took some effort to turn. Eventually McIntyre turned the last lock. The door was now open.

Out of the shadows a man suddenly appeared and attacked McIntyre from behind, it was one of The Shogun's bodyguards.

Emma screamed and turned to run away.

McIntyre pulled the man over his shoulder and onto the ground. The men wrestled in the dark.

There was a single loud bang followed by a bright flash of light as a gun was fired.

Emma stumbled and fell onto the dirt path, her nails dug deep into the damp cold ground, and she began to sob.

"Fergus!!" Emma cried out.

"I'm alright." replied McIntyre moving towards Emma, but he stopped abruptly.

The Shogun appeared behind Emma and held his gun directly to her head.

"Thank you, Emma for the history lesson, it was very interesting. Amusing stories about your petty little country. Thank you also for unlocking the door McIntyre. I really couldn't have done it without you." said The Shogun mockingly.

"Now, McIntyre dispose of your gun over there." said The Shogun pointing to a dark corner.

McIntyre could have easily shot The Shogun, but it was a risk he could not take. His sisters' life was in danger. He did as The Shogun requested. Emma stood up slowly and the Shogun ordered them both back to the door.

"Interesting how the Americans called it a red gate, is it not?" asked The Shogun.

"You see, a red gate in Japan is an entrance to a sacred space." explained The Shogun.

"Also!" said The Shogun, "The diagonal cross, it has another meaning in Japanese you know. It means …"

"Batsu." interrupted McIntyre.

"Yes," said The Shogun, surprised McIntyre knew what it meant.

"It means punishment." explained McIntyre.

"Right again Mr McIntyre. Very appropriate don't you think." said The Shogun now laughing.

"I've been studying your history and culture for quite some time now. Here's another interesting fact for you. The motto above the gatehouse at Edinburgh castle 'Nemo Me Impune Lacessit'. Tell us what it means Emma, I'm dying to hear the answer." insisted The Shogun.

"I'm …I'm not sure." said Emma faltering.

"Oh, come now. Surely a clever girl like you knows her Latin." scoffed The Shogun.

"It's 'No one provokes me with impunity'." blurted out McIntyre.

"Once again Mr McIntyre you are correct. Well, I'm not surprised you know that really. You see Emma, the motto is used by several army regiments in Scotland and other military groups around the world." explained The Shogun.

There was a long silence then The Shogun continued speaking. "… 'No one provokes me with impunity'." said The Shogun repeating the words.

"Or a better way of saying it, no one attacks me unpunished!" The Shogun seethed.

"Well, today I get my revenge and the West will be punished!" yelled The Shogun.

McIntyre interrupted The Shogun and spoke to him in Japanese. "Yamete kudasai. Hiroshima de okotta koto wa saigaideshita. Subete no Nihon to sekai no tame ni." *(Please stop. What happened at Hiroshima was a disaster. For all of Japan and the world.)*

"Mou Nidoto." *(Never again)* said McIntyre urging The Shogun to reconsider.

The Shogun fell silent. He looked at the ground then continued to speak.

"Very good McIntyre. I am impressed with your negotiating skills, but it is too late for negotiations. The West destroyed my country, my family, my people. They took everything!" The Shogun raged. "Now open the door, Emma!" he demanded.

Emma looked at her brother. McIntyre gave her a consenting nod, then with both hands and with all of her strength she heaved the heavy metal door open and stepped to one side.

"After you." The Shogun said now pointing the gun at both Emma and McIntyre.

McIntyre and Emma walked through the doorway and into the dark tunnel with The Shogun following close behind.

Reflecting on his long journey searching for the bombs, The Shogun couldn't quite believe he was finally here at last. He felt a sudden sense of relief. Now his plan for revenge was almost complete.

"Lead me to the bombs McIntyre." The Shogun demanded.

McIntyre held up the torch and started to walk slowly through the tunnel. Emma turned to look at The Shogun.

"Move!!" yelled The Shogun at Emma.

Emma jumped then stumbled forward, tripping over debris on the tunnel floor.

The steep incline of the tunnel was apparent as they walked further underground. With every step they took the rumbling sounds from above gradually dispersed, until the only noise heard was the crunch of the gravel below their feet.

Soon they could see remnants of cubicles made from bricks, once used as air raid shelters by thousands of people who gathered here for protection during the second world war.

McIntyre stopped and turned to face an archway.

"Are we here? Is this it?" asked The Shogun impatiently.

In his excitement The Shogun lowered his gun and walked towards the opening.

McIntyre seized his chance. He slapped the gun out of The Shogun's hand and tried to restrain him.

The Shogun quickly pressed a button on his walking stick. Two blades projected from the bottom of the shaft. Then he stabbed McIntyre in his foot with the blades.

McIntyre let out a painful scream, he dropped the torch and fell to the ground.

As the torch rolled away the light flashed on the tunnel walls, then suddenly it switched off, plunging them all into complete darkness.

"Fergus! Where are you?!" yelled Emma.

The Shogun made his escape and disappeared through the archway.

"Here Emma!" groaned McIntyre.

Emma scrabbled about on the dirty gravel floor and found the torch. She quickly turned it on to see McIntyre holding his wounded foot.

"Find the gun. It should be over there." McIntyre said pointing close to the archway.

Emma searched with the torch, waving the beam of light from side to side.

"Got it!" she shouted and ran back to her brother.

"We need to hurry." said McIntyre standing up

He took the gun from Emma.

"Where is that Rat?!" seethed McIntyre furiously and he limped forward through the archway.

Scurrying on through the gloomy narrow passage The Shogun came nearer to his dream. A small amount of light coming from a ventilation shaft helped guide him through the passage. The lack of light did not deter him, his eyesight had been deteriorating for years and he was accustomed to feeling his way around in the dark.

The Shogun stopped briefly and raised his arm to remove a mass of sticky cobwebs that had wrapped around his face. Unfazed he carried on through the passage. Gradually, more light appeared in front of him, he felt sure he was getting close.

The Shogun suddenly stopped. In front of him was an enormous manmade bunker. The cavernous space dropped down several meters from where he was standing.

In the dim light The Shogun could see discarded filing cabinets and out of date equipment scattered around the bunker. His eyes then fixed on something protruding just above the floor level, he saw what looked like a warhead.

The Shogun could hardly contain his excitement. He smiled and turned to descend a set of metal stairs on his left.

There was a loud gunshot.

The Shogun felt a hot sharp pain in his back and a cloud of blood burst through the front of his chest. His smile quickly disappeared from his face, and he turned around slowly to see the outline of a man standing in the shadows.

"Who are you?" whimpered The Shogun.

The man stepped forward into the light. It was McIntyre.

"I am Whitehall. Rotherhithe. Albert. Imperial. Thames. Hyde." answered McIntyre.

McIntyre paused for a moment then aimed his gun at The Shogun and pulled the trigger once more.

Standing over The Shogun's lifeless body McIntyre yelled the words, "I AM WRAITH!"

CHAPTER EIGHTEEN

ONE WEEK LATER
SCOTTISH NATIONAL GALLERY
EDINBURGH

On the road outside the Scottish National Gallery a large crowd gathered.

A sea of waving saltire flags swayed to the beat of banging drums and a continuous melodic tune from the drone of bagpipes soared through the air.

Photographers, television crew and reporters set up their equipment in front of the crowd. One reporter picked up his microphone and started communicating with the camera in front of him.

"We are here today in the city of Edinburgh, Scotland's capital city, to witness what might be one of the largest ever recorded marches for Scottish Independence. But before we get to that story, we have some new information to share with you on the situation that occurred here just last week. Gunfire at numerous locations in the city, which were thought to be gang related, have been revealed as an act of heroism as part of a top-secret operation ......"

....

McIntyre sat quietly on a leather chesterfield bench inside the gallery. He stared contently at a painting of a majestic stag. He wasn't much of an art lover, but the painting stirred some emotions in him.

Emma came to sit beside her brother. They sat in silence for a moment both taking in the impressive painting.

"They're making a bit of a racket out there aren't they. Still, I think it's great to see all the saltire flags waving and people being passionate about their country." said Emma.

She turned to her brother who was still staring at the painting.

"Well, you're not a wanted man anymore. But you'll have to account for your actions, and I suspect you will have to suffer the consequences." said Emma giving her brother one final reprimand.

McIntyre laughed. "I always do." he sighed.

"How's the foot?" asked Emma.

"Oh, fine. It stings a little, but I can live with it." replied McIntyre smiling.

"Good. Well, I better be getting back to my day job." said Emma. She tossed a set of car keys for the Lotus Evija at her brother.

"Keep it." Emma said smiling. "Come and visit me, won't you?" she asked.

Without waiting for an answer, Emma walked towards the door and out of the gallery.

McIntyre turned back to look at the painting then got up from the bench. As he stood up, he saw a man facing away looking at another painting.

McIntyre felt sure he recognised him, even though all he could see was the back of the man's head.

The air in the room seemed to get cooler the more McIntyre stared at the man. The change in temperature made the hairs on his arm stand up. He rubbed his arm to warm his body, then put his jacket on.

Looking over at the man once more McIntyre considered approaching him but dismissed his feelings and instead headed for the exit.

He had work to get back to and a lot of explaining to do. He also had a few unanswered questions of his own.

McIntyre recalled the conversation he had with Hitoshi confirming his suspicions that other criminal groups were involved. He wasn't entirely convinced this was over.

The unidentified man turned his head slightly. He did not look at McIntyre but was aware of his departure. The man then let out an icy sigh and quickly raised his hood over his head, ready for action.

....

Printed in Great Britain
by Amazon